Sherlock Holmes and The Mystery of the First Unicorn

I0546960

By
Lidia Svec
&
Joseph W. Svec III

Paperback ISBN 978-1-78705-343-4
ePub ISBN 978-1-78705-344-1
PDF ISBN 978-1-78705-345-8

Published in the UK by MX Publishing
335 Princess Park Manor, Royal Drive,
London, N11 3GX www.mxpublishing.com

Cover design by Brian Belanger – chapter header images by clipart.com.

The authors may be contacted via their web page, www.pixymuse.com or via their Facebook page www.facebook.com/sherlockgrinningcat.

Dedication

This book is dedicated to Laura Simmerman, friend, big sister extraordinaire, nurse, and Alaskan pioneer.

Sherlock Holmes
and the Mystery of the First Unicorn

Table of Contents:

Sherlock Holmes and the Mystery of the First Unicorn

A Note to Readers:

The following story, *Sherlock Holmes and the Mystery of the First Unicorn*, in truth, begins with the conclusion of the final events of the *Sherlock Holmes and the Missing Authors Trilogy*. While that trio of narratives is somewhat unusual by Sherlock Holmes' standards, this tale leads Holmes and Watson off on one of the most uncanny adventures ever recorded by the stalwart Doctor; a search to solve the disappearance of the very first unicorn ever to grace this planet.

Unicorns hold a special place in myth, legend, and literature. And as such, you may have preconceptions regarding this magnificent creature, based upon what you have already read on the subject. And it is highly possible, that they may differ from certain facts recorded by Dr. Watson. However, I assure you, that this manuscript is accurately reproduced, just as it was found.

As with the previous manuscripts, Dr. Watson had requested that this story not be published until seventy-five years after his passing. Once again, as this document was lost for many years and has just recently been recovered, the requested amount of time has more than passed, so this story may be published and presented for your consideration.

Prologue

Memorandum:
To: Whom it may Concern
From: Dr. John Watson M.D.
Subject: *Sherlock Holmes and the Mystery of the First Unicorn*
Date: February 1898

I have recorded many of the more notable and unusual cases of Sherlock Holmes, and as a result, have been accused of slight exaggerations, and perhaps at times, even sensationalism. However, as his close friend and biographer, I can assure you that the story contained in this manuscript is most certainly presented exactly as it occurred.

Having just completed a series of adventures involving missing authors and their literary characters coming to life from the pages of their novels, it seemed as if almost anything were possible. And it must be said, when a unicorn enters the equation, I assure you it certainly is. This tale is without question, the most unusual adventure of Sherlock's that I have recorded.

That being said, in consideration of Sherlock's reputation as a consulting detective, and to protect my own medical practice, I must request that this manuscript not be published until seventy-five years after my passing. Your compliance in honoring this request is appreciated.

Dr. John H. Watson MD

Sherlock Holmes
and the Mystery of the First Unicorn

Chapter 1.

An Explanation, of how Sherlock Holmes Found Himself Outwitted. (And by a mythical, supposedly nonexistent creature at that.)

I will be the first to say it. It is not very often that the great detective, Sherlock Holmes finds himself outwitted. Oh, I will say, that at times during some of his more challenging cases, he has been quite perplexed, temporarily stymied, or on infrequent occasions, at a total loss as to which direction to turn. However, no matter how long he sequesters himself in that private den of calculations, hidden deep within his cave of concentration, he has always rallied to the occasion, and come up with the right answer. After endless hours of utter silence, usually filled with the noxious fog of pipe tobacco, or occasionally endless violin music, he will suddenly stand up, and without a word of explanation, tell me to gather my coat and service revolver, and we will be off to bring another case to a successful conclusion.

During his stellar career, he has matched wits against some of England's most notoriously clever and devious criminal masterminds, and successfully out-thought, out-calculated, out-reasoned, out-played, out-foxed, and utterly vanquished them. During our *Adventure of the Grinning Cat,* he had even solved "the unsolvable" *ultimate* logic puzzle that was created by the Guardians of Time, themselves. So, you will see that it is with great reserve that I begin this adventure by stating that Sherlock Holmes had definitely been outwitted, and by a mythical, legendary creature, that most would say does not even exist. They would say that it was purely imaginary and stop right there. That would be the end, and it would be a rather brief narrative. But I can attest to you. I was there, and I witnessed the entire exchange. It was a genuine, real unicorn, that had accompanied us on a rather odd journey to save England's Poet Laureate, Alfred Lord Tennyson, and along the way assist the legendary King Arthur, and Merlin himself, in resolving certain issues with Morgan le Fey. Yes, I do understand. That sounds even less plausible than a real unicorn, but again, trust me, I was there. It was as real as could be imagined.

Actually, we had previously encountered a unicorn during our *Grinning Cat* adventure, but I had rationalized that entire experience, as a part of Lewis Carroll's Wonderland and its associated creatures coming to life as a result of Carroll's dealings with the Time Guardians. It made *logical* sense, as much as it possibly could, all things considered. That particular unicorn was one of Lewis Carroll's Wonderland characters from his novel, *Alice Through the Looking Glass.* Wonderland and its fictional inhabitants had been somehow brought into existence by the Time Guardians, which means the unicorn was also brought to life, so there you have it, a logical explanation for the presence of a live unicorn.

But, returning to the matter at hand, during *The Round Table Adventure,* Sherlock and I had actually, traveled back in time through a portal in the standing megaliths of Stonehenge, to the era of King Arthur and Camelot, and I assure you, that in that time period, unicorns, and even dragons, mind you, really did exist. While Sherlock was successfully able to deal with a multitude of less than logical situations, and unusual creatures of that era, and he continuously solved every challenge, conundrum, and enigma that we came across, at the very end, he apparently did let his guard down.

As we were preparing to return to present-day London, the unicorn had mentioned that he was trying to resolve the *"greatest unsolved mystery of all time,"* one that would be a significant challenge even for the great detective, Sherlock Holmes. Of course, Holmes casually dismissed the notion, saying that he could quickly solve the mystery in his spare time in between cases and that it would present no problem to him, whatsoever at all.

Interpreting Holmes' reply as an affirmative agreement, the unicorn then responded with profuse thanks and appreciation for Sherlock's offer to solve the mystery. The creature stated that it had been a great honor to assist Holmes in the matter of Lord Tennyson, and he would be even more honored, to have the assistance of Sherlock Holmes in solving this ultimate, unsolvable mystery. The unicorn then happily cantered off to make arrangements to accompany Sherlock and me back to present day London, to begin our new adventure. It is true, the creature had provided invaluable assistance in rescuing Alfred Lord Tennyson, and Sherlock did say that he could *quickly* solve the problem in between cases, with minimal effort, so the outwitted Sherlock Holmes reluctantly agreed to help solve *The Mystery of the First Unicorn.*

And that is how it came to be that we have a unicorn in the enclosed garden in back of Mrs. Hudson's Lodgings, here, at 221-B Baker Street, in present-day London. Fortunately, the garden is well sheltered, providing a goodly amount of privacy, and most people living today, having lost their sense of wonder and imagination, do not even notice the horn of the creature. (Excuse me, I have been corrected. The proper term for the horn of a unicorn is an *alicorn*. The unicorn is most particular about that particular point.) But as I was saying, most people just see a magnificent white horse. The few fortunate people who do see the unicorn for what it really is, are astounded, and count the day as one to remember for the rest of their lives. Late at night when tucking their children into bed, they get a starry-eyed far-off look, and mention the magical day that they actually saw a real live unicorn…

Of course, no one believes them. Now that it is all over, and the unicorn has returned to his own time, I sometimes wonder if Sherlock Holmes himself still believes. But as he had initially said, he could easily solve the mystery of the first unicorn "in between" his cases. He did make that stipulation, and there were a number of interesting clients and situations that came through the door of our lodgings while Sherlock was pursuing the long-lost secret of the very first unicorn.

In addition to the mystery of the first unicorn, I will share with the reader each of these small adventures, because as it turned out, oddly enough, each of these additional cases related in some way to the solving of the unicorn mystery. Like the threads of a medieval tapestry, they all wove together in a strange and unexpected way that revealed a picture, and an answer that none of us could have ever imagined.

And so, with that rather involved explanation, and introduction, I will begin this story by sharing an odd case that began almost as soon as we returned. And it nearly ended just as fast as it began, with Sherlock threatening to throw the client out the window!

Chapter 2.

The Case of the Missing Socks. (And Sherlock really puts his foot down.)

As you are already aware, Sherlock Holmes and I had just completed an odd adventure that had taken us back in time to medieval England, and we had returned with a real, live unicorn in tow. Mrs. Hudson, who has a fond affinity for that particular mystical creature, was happy to lead it out to the enclosed garden in back of her lodgings. It is a much more suitable environment for a Unicorn. Being that the month was February, and London was exhibiting its usual dreary winter gloom, I recall commenting, that she may have wanted to wear a shawl since it was quite chilly outside, but she oddly replied, that thanks to the Unicorn she was as warm as could be. At the time, I did not have the opportunity to consider her response, as we were interrupted by a loud and urgent knocking upon our door.

Sherlock casually commented, "I would hope that is not animal control. You do know, that we have had a rather large menagerie of assorted creatures here in the flat as a result of these last several cases, and I am certain, that unicorns in the garden, are not covered by municipal codes. Do open the door Watson and see who it is."

I opened the door, and a rather beleaguered and worried looking gentleman stood there before me.

"Are you Sherlock Holmes? You are the only one that can help me! Please!" he emphatically stated.

"No, I am his friend, and associate, Dr. John Watson. However, Sherlock Holmes is here at the moment. Please, do come inside."

"Thank you so much!" he responded, as he quickly hurried through the door. He was bespectacled, tall and slender, rather stark looking, with an inquisitive look about him. Though his grey eyes were bright and piercing, they showed signs of the significant strain he was evidently experiencing. His brown hair was unkempt, and he had what looked like several different chemical stains on the sleeves of his suit coat.

Sherlock looked the man over, and stated, "I see that you are a scientist, specializing in chemistry and physics. And you are also a mechanical engineer, who likes to take a hands-on approach to building things yourself, rather than letting your lab assistants do the physical work. In fact, I would say that you have no assistants, and you are very secretive about your efforts. You have come here to see me because some project of yours has gone missing. I am correct?"

The gentleman's eyes grew wide with amazement as he stood before Sherlock nodding vigorously. "Yes, yes, and yes again! Everything I have heard about you is true. I have not yet said a word about why I am here, and you have already stated half of the facts just by looking at me. How are you able to do that, Mr. Holmes?"

Sherlock with an air of indifference, as if he were explaining a basic mathematical equation to a beginners' class, elaborated. "It is all a matter of simple observation and seeing the obvious facts that the average person routinely misses. The chemical stains on your sleeves and slide rule in your pocket told me your profession. You have an engineer's toolkit attached to your belt. The scrapes on your knuckles, tell me you prefer to do the work yourself. Your nervous disposition and anxiety tell me that you generally trust no one but yourself, and you work entirely alone. The only reason someone, who matches all of the aforementioned characteristics, would come to see me, is if one your projects had gone missing. Now, would you care to share the rest of the facts pertaining to why you are here?"

The gentleman sighed, and nervously looked from Sherlock to me, and then back to Sherlock, "It's... rather *difficult* to explain, I was utterly shocked by what happened, and I am not exactly sure how to say this. I am rather embarrassed by the matter."

"Just tell us what it is," I prompted him. "We have helped numerous clients in many sensitive and unusual circumstances, and we will understand. You can have complete confidence in us."

He bowed his head and simply stated. "My socks have gone missing."

Sherlock clasped his hands together behind his head, turned to me and said, "Watson, please show this man the door immediately."

The gentleman started to stammer and tried to explain, but Sherlock stood up, pointed at the entrance, and in a loud clear voice, reiterated, "Watson get this person out of here before I throw him out the window myself! London's finest consulting detective does not locate missing socks!"

Upon hearing that, the man raised his voice, holding up his hands in desperation and exclaimed! "But you don't understand! They walked out of my laboratory of their own accord, with no one in them! They just walked out the door and vanished into the night. They were my project, a prototype of an important invention that I have been working on for weeks. You must help me retrieve them!"

I stopped in my tracks when I heard that and turned to Holmes who had also sat back down in his chair and replied, "Perhaps, I may have been just a bit premature in my judgment. Most unbecoming of me. Why don't you sit down and explain the exact nature of your project? Would you care for a cup of tea?"

Declining the offering of tea, the gentleman sat in the chair across from Sherlock, took a deep breath, and began to speak. "My name is Winfred Wilkinson. I am a scientist, and an engineer, as you surmised. My father is also an engineer, and as a result of several lucrative patents, our family is very well-to-do.

"He maintains a first-class research laboratory on Glentworth Street, not far from here, and his own machine shop, as well as a very extensive library. He is always acquiring new books. I must say, he almost enjoys devouring books more than he does food. Both of my parents read obsessively. They have stated on more than one occasion, that there is much truth to be found in the journals of ages past, and that a great deal of what has been considered myth and legend, may, in fact, be real."

Thinking back to our recently completed trip to the mythical and legendary city of Camelot I looked at Sherlock, and smiled, but said nothing.

"As a result of an odd reference in one of the old journals he had just purchased, my parents left rather quickly on an expedition a year ago and have not yet returned. They were in search of a secret that he stated, would revolutionize the world in both science and medicine. He never explained exactly what it was, just that it was unique, would be exceedingly hard to find, and might take quite some time to locate. He left me fully in charge of his laboratory and machine shop. That has allowed me the freedom to choose my own projects to work on."

"Such as the disappearing socks?" Sherlock ventured. "An interesting concept, I am sure. What else were they supposed to do?"

Winfred coughed and went on. "They were not supposed to disappear like that. That was never a part of their design. I am sure you are familiar with Ruhmkorff lamps, the portable hand cranked lanterns used in mines and cave exploring. Jules Verne even included them in his novel, *A Journey to the Center of the Earth*."

Recalling our recent adventure with both Jules Verne and Captain Nemo of the Nautilus, Sherlock and I just looked at each other and nodded. "We are familiar with Mr. Verne and his work," Sherlock replied. "Pray continue."

"Well with my parents off on an expedition to who knew where, it had occurred to me that countless explorers had frozen to death in the Arctic and Antarctic, or in the upper elevations of the world's highest peaks. What if the same concept as that of the Ruhmkorff lamps could be used in articles of clothing? But instead of generating light, they generated heat? Think of it! If you wear clothes that generate their own warmth, and you can safely go anywhere, in any kind of weather!"

Sherlock considered the idea and nodded, as our guest went on speaking.

"It took me quite some time to develop a wire that could be woven into clothing, be pliable and light enough to wear, and yet still provide enough heat to be useful, but I did it! I will spare you the details, but my first prototype article of clothing was a pair of socks. They were light blue in color. Think of all the frost-bitten feet that could be saved. The best part was that the coil that charged them was less than half the size of those used in the original Ruhmkorff lamps, and you could disconnect the charging wire. Once you heat up the socks, you could unplug them from the coil, so they were easier and less cumbersome to wear. I never expected them to walk out of my lab."

Sherlock leaned forward and asked, "Can you explain that part in detail? Try to describe it exactly as it occurred. Take your time to gather your thoughts and visualize the event before you begin. I have written a paper on the practice of visualization, as I find it very useful. If you would like to read it someday, the title is *A Step-by-Step Guide to Using Visualization as a Tool in Clearly Recalling any Given Event, focusing on the Improbable, and Difficult to Describe, due to its Perceived Improbability*. It really does make a difference."

Winfred stared blankly at Sherlock, shook his head briefly and then replied, "I am certain it would, but it is not necessary.

That moment is something I will never forget. It was only a day ago that I was running tests to see how long their heat held up while the socks were in extreme conditions, using blocks of ice to maintain the cold temperature. I had stepped away from the test area to retrieve a notepad, and as I was returning to the room, there was a rush of wind, a white blur, and the socks seemed to just get up and rush out the door of the lab, and then they disappeared down the street. I was at a total loss as to what to do. I have not mentioned this project to anyone, so I cannot imagine how anybody found out about it or would want to steal it. I made some enquiries as to who could possibly help me and was directed to you."

Holmes sat quietly for a moment considering, when Mrs. Hudson entered the room with a tray of teacups and a steaming pot of Earl Grey, saying, "My, my, it is a bit nippy out there. Would you gentlemen care for a spot of tea to take the chill off the morning?" I will be outside in the garden if you need anything else." She set the tray down on the table and left the room, after which we heard the back door open and close.

Winfred looked at Holmes and continued. "I know it is not much to go on, but that is all I can tell you. What do you think? Can you help me recover them?"

Sherlock stood up, walked over to the window overlooking the garden, and stared silently for only a minute, when he abruptly said, "If you will excuse me for just a moment." And he walked over to the door and left the room.

The gentleman stared at me with a questioning look and asked, "Was it something I said, or is that a typical response?"

I, being equally confused, replied saying, "Sherlock Holmes does not always explain himself when he gets an idea, but I am certain that he will be able to assist you in some way."

Within very little time, Holmes re-entered the room and addressed his client. "Mr. Wilkinson, Your case is resolved. In fact, by the time you return to your lab, you will find your Ruhmkorff socks have been returned to the test station none the worse for their unexpected stroll down the street. It has been a pleasure meeting you, even if I did threaten to throw you out the window. For that, I will wave my usual fee. Good day sir."

Mr. Wilkinson, of course, was totally taken aback. "I, I, don't know what to say. They will really be back in my lab by the time I return? That is wonderful! I had heard that you were the best, but this is truly amazing! Your skills defy science, itself. Thank you so very much! Once the prototype has finished testing and they are available, I will be sure to send you the first pair. Thank you again!"

And with that, he exited our flat, while Sherlock stood in silence, again staring out the window. I sat there waiting for an explanation, but in his usual manner, he did not say a word. Finally, I could no longer stand the suspense, so I queried him, "Holmes, are you, or are you not, going to tell me what just happened? How is it possible that the socks will be back in his laboratory by the time he returns? All you did is go out to the garden…"

It was then that it all dawned on me. Mrs. Hudson's comment about being warm thanks to the unicorn, the gust of wind and a *white* blur when the socks vanished, and again, Mrs. Hudson being outside without a shawl, and finally Sherlock's brief visit to the garden. I pointed out the window

15

towards the yard and asked, "Are you going to tell me that the unicorn took the socks and gave them to Mrs. Hudson?"

Just at that moment, the unicorn reentered the room saying, "Alright, they are right back where I found them, but I still don't understand why. What is the sense of leaving a heated pair of socks on a block of ice when your dear landlady, Mrs. Hudson can put them to much better use? They could keep her quite warm while she tends to her lovely garden."

Sherlock shook his head and replied. "But that is not the point. Sitting there unattended, does not mean they are free for the taking. One simply does not do that. It is not considered proper behavior. There are rules of society in this time period that simply must be obeyed."

The unicorn responded, "If you insist. I see this historical era will take some time to get accustomed to. And I thought your mechanical dragons were strange."

"But how did you even know about the socks?" I asked. "We just now returned today."

The unicorn tossed his head casually and replied. "When I transported King Arthur and his queen to your lodgings as part of Wizard Holmes' plan to capture Morgan le Fey, I noticed that Mrs. Hudson was chilled when she was outside working in her garden. The sensory abilities of unicorns are so exact, that even at a distance I was able to detect the heat being given off by a pair of socks that just happened to be laying unattended on a block of ice. That made no sense to me when she could obviously use them, and you saw that she really appreciated them."

Sherlock waved a hand dismissively. "Yes, yes. You have already explained that part. I do understand. When his invention goes into production, and we receive the promised samples, I will make sure Mrs. Hudson gets the first pair.

The unicorn nodded its head and replied, "That sounds agreeable. And since you have solved this case so quickly, and proven you can even locate a missing pair of socks, are you ready to begin our search for the first unicorn?

Chapter 3.

A Brief History of Unicorns. (And from the most reliable source imaginable, all things considered.)

Sherlock poured a steaming cup of tea, inhaled the fragrance of Mrs. Hudson's finest Earl Grey, sat down in his chair and stated, "Why don't you tell me what you know about the subject, so we have somewhere to start? It will be good to hear it 'direct from the horse's mouth,' so to speak, that is."

The unicorn snorted, and its eyes grew wide at Sherlock's comment, and he began, "Well, first of all, unicorns are not merely horses with horns. We are a separate and distinct species that was the first animal named by Adam. That is why our place in history, and our connection with humanity, has always been so special. Even though he could have remained in the garden when humankind was cast from it, the first unicorn chose to follow Adam and Eve into the world, to watch over them. The bond between early humanity and the unicorn was magical and timeless.

"It is thought that later when the great deluge occurred, the unicorns missed the boat so to speak, but it is much more complex than that. Unicorns are unique creatures in that we can transcend dimensions. Our form is transmutable if you understand me. That is why in different lands and cultures, the unicorn has been described quite differently. In the Far East, the unicorn is called the Ki-Lin, and their depictions look nothing like me. The same goes for the Persian unicorn, known as the Karkadamn, or the many other descriptions from around the world throughout the course of history.

"When the Earth was covered by the great flood, the unicorn became a sea creature. I believe humans refer to it as a narwhal. When the waters eventually receded, the unicorn did revert to its original form and return to the land.

"But how can that be?" I interrupted, "There are still narwhals living in the oceans."

The unicorn gazed out the window for a moment as if pondering and replied. "Well, yes that is true. There are still narwhals in the seas of the world. They would be the offspring of the first unicorn from the time he was in the ocean. It was their home since birth, and they chose to remain."

Sherlock looked up, casually raising a pointed finger and interjected, "*If* I may ask; if the first unicorn was a he, then how did he have offspring without a she? Are we searching for one or two unicorns?

The unicorn nodded and answered, "An excellent question. You are most observant. The Creator, in his infinite love and wisdom, did provide a mate to the first unicorn. That much is known, as is the fact that they both returned from the sea after the great deluge ended and the waters receded.

"Unicorns were granted an exceptionally long lifespan. While they are incredibly swift and can be formidable in combat when needed, their alicorn is a source of healing and purification. That is why their offspring both on land and in the ocean have been hunted for their horns. The foolish humans do not realize that the alicorn does not retain any powers if it is not a part of a living unicorn."

"It saddens me to think of the many unicorns that have died at the hands of misdirected humans, but fortunately, there have been many more humans over the ages that have protected and honored unicorns as well."

I interrupted him to ask if perhaps the first unicorn could have been killed by a hunter. Was that a possibility? That would explain why he just vanished.

"No, the death of a creature of such significance would be strongly felt among our species. I am certain of that. He and his mate somehow simply vanished near the end of the middle ages and have not been seen or felt since that time. We can sense the presence of another of our species, and even during the times when there does not seem to be any in existence, one unicorn would know if there are any others, somewhere in hiding. That is why this is such a great mystery. And that is why I needed the assistance of a great detective. So, what do you think, Wizard Holmes? Can you solve the mystery of the first unicorn? The stories of many unicorns have been immortalized in collections of medieval tapestries. Two of the most famous tapestry collections are the story of *The Lady and the Unicorn*, and the infamous, *The Hunt of the Unicorn*.

Perhaps the *Mystery of the First Unicorn* will be woven into a tapestry someday,"

Sherlock sat silently staring at the creature for a moment, pondering the information provided, before inquiring, "Can you tell me more about the transcending dimensions and transmutable forms that you mentioned? You were rather brief and vague about that."

The unicorn appeared to blur for a moment, and then materialized as what he later described as the Far Eastern Ki-Lin. He changed again and took the form of the Indian unicorn, and several other descriptions from unicorn lore as well. Then he seemed to just vanish before our eyes. Sherlock and I stared into the emptiness when we heard the unicorn's voice echoing from the other side of the room.

"You do realize, that I am still in this room. A unicorn, being very connected to the Earth, and the spirit of nature, can assume the form that is most acceptable to the time and culture that it exists in, and we can be invisible if required. However, I am still present physically even if you cannot see me."

Sherlock then turned toward the breakfast table and stated, "You do not need to be visible for me to be aware that you are now standing next to the table and about to consume the plate of muffins. Even invisible, there are at least a half a dozen indicators that tell me your physical location and intended action."

I turned to look, and the unicorn has reappeared right next to the breakfast table. I also noticed that several of the flatbread muffins had indeed vanished.

"Once again, Wizard Holmes, your powers of observation are truly outstanding, even if you are inside and sitting. So, from what I have shared, do you have any idea what could have happened to the first unicorn?"

Holmes was about to reply when the there was a loud knocking on the door, and the unicorn again vanished, as did the remainder of the flatbread muffins.

Chapter 4.

The Case of the Missing Lochs. (And we learn more about a unicorn's dry sense of humor.)

"We apparently have a visitor and prospective client, Watson. Would be so kind, as to open the door? We do not receive many visitors from Scotland," Sherlock remarked as he reached for a bottle of fine Scotch whiskey that he had stored in the tantalus.

I opened the door and was astounded to behold a tall, bearded gentleman, dressed in a kilt and full Scottish Highland attire, and carrying a walking stick, standing before me. Without thinking I turned to Sherlock and exclaimed, "Holmes, how could you possibly have known our visitor is from Scotland before I even opened the door?"

Holmes chided me and responded, "Watson, you should know my abilities by now. Do invite our guest in. He has traveled a great distance to seek my assistance and is most likely rather thirsty."

The gentleman upon hearing Holmes' reply marched into the room and commented, "Aye, that I have. And I can do with a wee drop o' that fine beverage you have oe'r there."

Much to our surprise, he pointed not at the bottle of Scotch, but at the tea service on the table.

"I do hope tha' is Mrs. Hoodson's Earl Grey Cream Tea on the table there. I ha' heard so mooch about it. It wa' King Arthur's favorite tea, you know. O'course it wa' the only tea he ever tasted, and tea as a beverage didna' even exist when he was alive, but that didna' stop him from writing about it."

Now, I was even more bewildered, than I was when Sherlock predicted our visitor's nationality before I opened the door. How could this gentleman possibly have known about our little adventure with King Arthur and Camelot. We had not mentioned it to anybody. And I knew Mrs. Hudson would not have told anyone. How was it possible?

Shaking his head and muttering something about no accounting for some people's taste in beverages, Sherlock returned the bottle of Scotch to the tantalus. He strode towards the table with the tea service, commenting, "Yes, actually that is Earl Grey Cream Tea, but if you don't mind my asking, how is it possible that you are even aware of it, or that King Arthur might have held it in such high regard?"

"First things first!" exclaimed the visitor as he thrust his walking stick and cloak into my hand, crossed over to the tea service in great strides, and reverently accepted the cup of tea that Sherlock offered him. He deeply inhaled the aroma of the steaming beverage, closed his eyes as if in a trance, and then slowly exhaled. "Ah, indeed, it may be called Earl Grey Cream, but this is surely the king o' teas. There is none other like it." He then slowly sipped the cup until it was empty, broke into a broad smile, handed the cup back to Sherlock requesting a refill, and stated, "Now we can begin!"

He accepted the second cup, crossed over to a chair, sat down and began. "Gentlemen, I imagine you ha' some questions. Actually, I too am a wee bit curious as to how you knew I hail from the Heelands before your associate opened the door. It can'a be me accent, as I had no yet said a word."

Sherlock waved his hand dismissively and replied. "I heard you coming up the stairs. As you walked, your kilt brushed against the wall, and it is a little-known fact that every different type of fabric makes a distinct and unique sound when brushing against a hard surface. I knew it was a Highlands woolen tartan just from the sound it made. Your walking stick also gave you away when you used it to knock on our door. I performed a comprehensive analysis titled, "*A Study of the Unique Acoustical Characteristics of Walking Sticks Knocking on Doors*," and I can state for a fact, that your cane was made by James MacLeish, of Glasgow, Scotland. That plus the subtle, yet unmistakable sound of your kilt, told me without question that you are from Scotland. Now if you can explain why you are here, I am certain that it is not only to sample Mrs. Hudson's Earl Grey Cream tea."

The gentleman drained his second cup, set it on the table, and continued. "To savor this tea alone, t'would be reason enough to mae' the journey, but no, that is no' the primary purpose of my visit. My name is McTavish. My lochs have gone missing, and I need you locate them."

At that point, he paused, gazed at the ceiling briefly, stared intently at us for a moment, and then continued. "There are more than thirty-one thousand lochs, or as you folks would call them, freshwater lakes, in Scotland, with most of them bein' found in the Heelands. As of just recently, there are two less than only a few weeks ago. And both of them vanished from my properties."

At that point, I cleared my throat and asked him, "Wouldn't this be a question for a geologist, or perhaps a civil engineer, and not a detective? How could someone possibly steal a freshwater lake, much less two of them? It just doesn't seem possible."

Sherlock then interjected, "Just a moment, Watson, let us hear more on this." And turning to our visitor he asked, "Can you explain the history or background of the lochs that vanished? And perhaps any recent changes in their nature just before they disappeared? That would be useful."

The gentleman pointed at Sherlock and exclaimed, "It is funny tha' you should mention that. I mean about recent changes in their nature. But I am getting ahead o' me self. They had been there for ages, eons I'm sure. They were not large, really. Some wou' call them only ponds, but they were on oor' family land. Well, one o'them was. The other sat right on oor' property line, but we called them lochs and lochs they were.

"Now, this next part may seem a wee bit strange to you. Oer' the years, rumors and legends were told that a unicorn lived in the vicinity o' the lochs. I never believed the stories, myself, but I will say that oor' family maintained excellent health, and some said that it wa' the unicorn that gave the water a healing touch. In fact, just this year an engineer and his wife came to me asking about the waters and unicorns, and such. I don' know how he found ou' about it, but he mentioned having recently read something in an ol' journal. His wife was ailing badly at the time, and after bathing in the loch's water, she was fine again. When I saw that, I thought to myself; this can make me a wee bit o' money.

"I had some signs made up proclaiming the healing nature o' the water, and wa' ready to start charging a fee to bathe in the lochs, and the next day, the lochs were gone! Vanished! It was no like they ha' dried up, and there wa' a dry lake bed. It wa' like they were neva' there!"

When he mentioned that, I would have sworn, I heard a muffled snickering from where the unicorn had last been standing. Even the visitor turned and looked in that direction and asked, "Might there be soomone else here? I am sure I just heard a voice." To which Sherlock smiled and dismissively replied, "I assure you, there are no other persons in the room beyond yourself and Dr. Watson. Pray do continue. This is most fascinating."

"Well, I don' know wha' else to say. They were there for ages and now they're gone. And so is the fine purse o' coin they cou' ha' brought in."

Sherlock folded his fingers in front of him and asked, "Now you stated, that you did not believe the old stories of a unicorn in the vicinity of the lochs, but what about your ancestors, what did they have to say about it?"

"It wa' said that they honored the beast, by leaving fresh vegetables by the shore o' the lochs, and in the morning, they'd be gone. But any creature could o' ate them. Really, it wa' just an ol' story. I am certain o' that."

27

Sherlock nodded his head, saying, "Yes, yes… If you don't mind my changing the subject, when you first entered the room, you commented about King Arthur enjoying Earl Grey Cream Tea, even though tea did not appear in England until several hundred years after the reign of King Arthur. Would you mind explaining how you came across that bit of information? It may actually be pertinent to this case."

The Scotsman gave a surprised look and answered. "My clan is quite ol', and oor' ancestors date ba' to Arthur's time. It is tol' that one was a knight o' the roun' table. A prized family heirloom, that's been passed down through the ages, is a scroll said to have been written by King Arthur himself. I don' know how that can be, since he talks abou' a unicorn, and his love o' a beverage he called Mrs. Hoodson's Earl Grey Cream Tea, especially since unicorns are mythical creatures, and tea did na' exist ba' then, but it makes a great story to tell a' clan gatherings. I had heard so much abou' the tea, and then I foun' out abou' your landlady being called Mrs. Hoodson, I ha' to try it since I was here anyway. It truly is marvelous, the best tea I ha' ever tasted!"

Fortunately, he was looking away and did not see the teapot floating through the air, heading his direction seemingly of its own accord from the location of where the unicorn had last been standing. I managed to grab the teapot from the invisible creature before it clobbered our visitor in the head. As McTavish turned towards me, I casually asked him if he would care for some more tea. He looked a bit startled but answered that he would certainly enjoy another cup.

After pouring it, Sherlock and I stared at each other silently. Maybe his little escapade in Camelot was more significant than we had imagined.

Sherlock then broke the silence saying, "Yes, that would explain it. Returning to the subject of your missing lochs and unicorns, let me ask you a question. This may sound rather strange, and a week ago I would not have even considered it possible myself. However, it seems to me like your ancestors believed in the presence of a unicorn on your lands, and they honored it, providing food on a regular basis, and in return, a unicorn freely bestowed a healing power to the waters of your lochs that were present until you were about to charge for the use of it to make a profit. A bit of 'dry humor' on the part of the creature. Would you not agree?"

The Scotsman stood up and exclaimed, "Do ya think me daft?" and was about to continue when his face went white, and his eyes grew wide, and he stopped abruptly. He slumped back into his chair, whispering, "It canna be… It simply canna be…"

I turned and looked and noticed that the unicorn had briefly materialized for a moment, and then vanished just as quickly. He then pointed directly at the empty space, with a look of confusion, and stammering, asked, "Did ya see tha'? Please tell me you saw tha'! Or am I the one that's really going daft?"

Sherlock patted him lightly on the hand and answered. "I assure you. What you saw, really was there, and would explain why your lochs vanished. I imagine, that if you return home and take down the signs and begin carrying on the tradition of your ancestors in leaving fresh greens for the unicorn, you may see that in time, your lochs will return just as mysteriously as they vanished."

Just then there was a white blur and a quick breeze, and Sherlock added, "In fact, I have it from a most reliable source, that if you follow my instructions, your lochs will most certainly be back where they have always been."

The gentleman stood and incredulously replied, "I don' na know what to say. You are truly amazing. Did I really see a... well, you know...was it really there? Oh, I promise you, the signs will be taken down as soon as I return. An' I'll leave the finest greens that I can lay me hands on."

As he exited the door and went down the stairs, he continued to thank us, and shook his head saying, "That was amazing! Truly amazing!"

As I closed the door, the unicorn reappeared and commented. "You do realize, that you neglected to charge him a fee for solving this case."

Chapter 5.

Some Additional Notes About Unicorns. (And once again, from the most knowledgeable of sources. But I wouldn't put it past Sherlock to write a paper on it.)

Sherlock just leaned back in his chair, smiled, and replied, "Seeing the expression on his face, when he saw you, was worth more than any amount I could have charged him."

Sherlock sighed and stated. "This little adventure may be more intriguing than I first imagined. Did you notice anything unusual about our visitor's story that seemed particularly pertinent to our current endeavor?"

I nodded my head in agreement and replied, "He mentioned an engineer and his wife turning up at his lochs because of something they had read in an old journal. That means they must be the father and mother of your previous client with the missing socks. It makes perfect sense. It is rather amazing that the two cases should be connected like that. Wouldn't you agree?"

"Watson, you know I hesitate to jump to conclusions prematurely, but it would almost assuredly seem to be them. To be absolutely certain, I really should verify by consulting my little monograph on *How to Avoid making Incorrect Assumptions, Assessments, and Otherwise Embarrassing Statements by Jumping to Hasty Conclusions without Sufficient Information, Data, and Analysis, with an Emphasis on Considering the Trifling bits of Information that are Always Ignored.*"

At that moment, the unicorn shook its head incredulously and asked, "Was that the title of it, or the entire paper? Have you considered shortening the name any? Something simple, like *Look Before you Leap*?"

This time it was my turn to disagree. "That phrase has already been used. It is quite common actually."

The unicorn thoughtfully replied, "Well, in that case, call it, *Before you leap, look.*" Then squinting its eyes and staring intently, it added, "*and very closely*, at that."

Sherlock interrupted, "Regardless of what I call it, the two aspects do align very closely. Based on an old journal, Mr. Winfred's parents left to search for something that would revolutionize science and medicine and would be difficult to locate. And it was an engineer and his wife that seemed to have some awareness of unicorns and the healing properties of Mr. McTavish's lochs."

Sherlock turned to the unicorn, and asked, "Can you expound a bit more on the ability of the unicorn to impart a healing nature to water?"

Rearing up and striking a regal pose just for a moment, the unicorn replied. "It has been written by the king's surgeon, Ambroise Pare' in the 1500s, as well as the apothecaries, Andrea Bacci and Laurent Catelan of the same era, that the unicorn horn, or alicorn, as it is more properly called, has many healing functions. It was well known in the time of Arthur, that if a serpent or viper had poisoned a lake or pond, that just by immersing the alicorn into the water, the unicorn would purify it. Of course, it must be still attached to a living unicorn to work." He added with a slight nod of his head and then continued. "All of the animals in the area would wait until the unicorn had come and made the water safe to drink.

"The long-term presence of a unicorn in the vicinity of the lochs on the Scotsman's land would explain why his lochs have curative properties. Over time they would absorb some of that healing energy. I am not surprised that the unicorn caused them to appear to have vanished, when McTavish was going to charge people to use what was freely given. As you said, a rather amusing bit of dry humor."

"In addition to purifying water and healing, the alicorn is also able to detect poisons. In fact, most medieval kings kept powdered unicorn horn on hand at all times, and it was an essential part of every meal. However, as I previously stated, it does not function very long without the rest of a living unicorn. Some residual healing effect is present in the alicorn, but it eventually does fade. In spite of that, many apothecaries of ages past used the symbol of the unicorn for their shop signs.

To which Sherlock replied, "That would explain the relatively short life spans of many kings of that era if they were relying on a nonfunctional antidote artifact."

33

Then changing the subject, I asked," I am curious if the couple that turned up at McTavish's property were Wilkinson's parents, how could they possibly have known about the lochs in Scotland? I wonder who it was that recorded the information in the journal, and what additional clues it might contain."

With a look of clarity in his eyes and sharp determination, Sherlock grinned and affirmed, "Indeed, Watson, indeed. What other pertinent clues might that journal contain? That is the question of the moment, and if we are to make any progress in this adventure, it is one that must be answered. I shall return presently. Don't go away.

And with that, he grabbed his coat, walking stick, and deerstalker hat, and promptly left the room. He apparently left the premises, as we heard his footsteps going down the stairs, the door opening and closing, and Sherlock Holmes exiting into a cold and overcast London afternoon.

Chapter 6.

The Case of the Missing Rocks. (And Sherlock makes an important discovery, even if he says it was only a trifle.)

Sherlock Holmes had suddenly left the flat, to pursue a thought he had pertaining to the mysterious journal, which might contain additional clues in the mystery of the first unicorn. He did not say where he was going, or what he had expected to find. So, I was left with the unicorn, who was now devouring the rest of the muffins and going on, in great detail, about the dietary habits of unicorns throughout history. Needless to say, I was wondering what to do until he returned.

My pondering was thankfully short-lived, as I heard a faint sound of footsteps on the stairs, followed by a very slight tapping on the door, almost as if the person knocking were afraid of being heard. As the unicorn faded into invisibility, I arose and answered the door, and found myself utterly astonished by the appearance of the lady who stood before me!

It was as if I were gazing into the eyes of Luna, a mesmerizing, and enchanting mermaid, that I had met during the course of our Nautilus adventure. That fascinating journey had begun when Captain Nemo called upon Sherlock to enlist his help in locating Jules Verne, who had been kidnapped. Along the way. I had met the mermaid, and I must confess, became altogether infatuated with her beauty, and charming personality. As strongly as I had felt about her, due to the fact that she was a real, live, honest-to-goodness mermaid, and confined to an aquatic existence, it was simply not meant to be. I had sadly resolved myself to never seeing her again. Yet, here she was standing before me. How could it be? It was a dream come true.

Or was it? As I stared at her, like a love-struck schoolboy, I started to notice slight and very subtle differences between the lady's appearance and my cherished memory of Luna. They both had nearly identical, stunning, softly sculpted faces, beautiful long dark hair, and the deepest most captivating eyes. But while Luna's eyes were an intense azure blue, the lady standing before me had eyes of an almost a greyish purple color. I was observing other slight differences, when she coughed, and softly asked, if she could come in.

I recovered my senses and apologized, saying, "Yes, yes, please do come in. I am quite sorry for my lack of courtesy. It is just that you very much reminded me of someone else."

With a slight glance back towards me as she entered, she coyly replied, "Judging by the way you stared, she must have been someone extraordinary. I accept your apology. Are you Mr. Sherlock Holmes?"

I clumsily offered her a chair, and stammered a reply, "Uh, No, Sherlock is not here at the moment, but he may be back quite soon if you would care to wait. May I offer you a cup of tea? We have some already made. My name is Doctor John Watson. I assist Sherlock in many of his cases. Can I be of any help to you, Miss…?" I left the question open, hoping to learn her name, and perhaps something more about her.

As she sat quietly considering my question, I continued to notice the similarities and the differences between her and my beloved Luna. They were both slight of build with elegant and delicate features that had enchanted me yet exhibited a strength of character and forcefulness if needed. I found myself feeling a strong attraction to her and was wondering what brought her here when she answered in a voice that was soft and gentle yet exhibited a remarkable clarity.

"My name is Miss Leeda, and I am an explorer, seeker, and collector of crystalline formations of unique manifestations from the mineral realm, as well as an interpreter of how they communicate Mother Earth's message to our consciousness. And yes, thank you, a cup of tea would be lovely."

I stared at her rather blankly, when I heard the unicorn's voice whispering in my ear, "What she is saying, is that she is a geologist and a rather mystically inclined one at that. Are you going to pour her some tea, or would you like me to do it?"

The unicorn, still invisible, had again picked up the teapot, which I hastily grabbed, hoping she had not noticed it somehow "floating." I poured our guest a cup of tea and handed it to her. As I did, I nodded, and answered, "I see, and how can Sherlock Holmes, or I, be of any help to you?"

She sipped her tea, and replied, "While women are generally unwelcome and uncommon in scientific endeavors, there have been those of us who have nevertheless managed to make a significant foray into scholarly fields. Perhaps you have heard of Mary Anning, who died in 1847. She was a well-known fossil collector and paleontologist from Dorset County. She made many important finds in the Jurassic marine fossil beds, located in the cliffs of the English Channel at Lyme Regis."

I gazed out the window briefly and tried to recall the name when it came to me. "Yes. Wasn't she the lady fossil dealer, who made quite a name for herself selling dinosaur bones or something?"

Miss Leeda gave me a rather severe look and replied, "Mary Anning was much more than a dealer in dinosaur bones. She knew more about ancient species than many of the so-called 'experts' she sold her specimens to. But that is not why I am here. As I stated, I too am a scientist and collector of geological examples. Up until a year ago, I had been working in a remote area of Scotland, gathering some rather unique fluorite specimens near a pair of small lochs. I had returned to London to consult with a colleague of mine, and before returning to the dig site, my backpack was stolen. It contained several significant mineral specimens and…"

At that moment the door to the flat was suddenly flung open, revealing Sherlock Holmes, brandishing a number of sheets of handwritten notepaper, and continuing her sentence as if he had been in the room the entire time, "… and even more importantly, your personal journal of the discoveries and your work at that site. Here is a copy of your journal ma'am."

Miss Leeda and I both turned and exclaimed at the same time, "But how could you have possibly known that? And where did you get those copies?"

Sherlock handed the papers to our client, who was most happy to receive them, then he turned to me and replied with an air of casual indifference, "Really Watson, isn't it obvious? It was just a trifle. A mere snippet of a trifle, I tell you. This is a duplicate of the very same journal that our previous two clients had mentioned. The clues were obvious, and any scientist with information as valuable as that contained in this journal, would most certainly have made a backup copy before leaving on a long and perhaps perilous journey. I simply paid a visit to Mr. Wilkinson's lab and explained that his parents had without question left a duplicate behind and that I needed to borrow it. He was most enthusiastic and appreciative for our help. By the way, his heated socks were safely back in his lab as I had predicted. He was quite cooperative, even if he did not have a clue as to where it might have been hidden. It took only a moment of observing and analyzing his work area, for me to deduce exactly where the copies had been stored away."

He paused to pour himself a cup of tea, and introduce himself to Miss Leeda, who was understandably somewhat astonished.

"My journal and crystal specimens have been missing for more than a year now. How is it even conceivable that you could walk through the door with a copy of it on the very day that I come to engage your services to recover it? That doesn't even seem possible!"

Sherlock patted the hand of Miss Leeda, and said, "I think you had better sit down while I share with you the information behind how I came into the possession of this copy." He then took a seat in the chair across from her and continued. "I assure you, some parts of this explanation will be considerably more difficult to accept, than my having a copy of it at this specific moment in time. But as your journal has become an integral part of the case that I am currently pursuing, you will need to know certain less-than plausible facts."

Regaining her composure, she calmly set her teacup down on the table and asked, "Would that be that I saw the owner of the land containing the two lochs near where I have been working for the last several years, leaving your office just as I was arriving? Or is it perhaps the presence of a real unicorn here in your office? Is there anything else you would like to share?"

This time, I stared wide-eyed at Sherlock in utter surprise, and when the unicorn reappeared, with its magnificent white coat almost glowing, and its spiral horn positively radiating light, Miss Leeda just nodded at it and smiled.

Chapter 7.

Several Different Paths Converge and then Diverge. (But Sherlock has an idea that may provide a solution.)

I must confess, I was even more confounded by Miss Leeda's statements and her somehow being aware of the intangible unicorn's presence than Sherlock's sudden return with a copy of the mysterious journal. "Can someone please explain what exactly is going on here?" I exclaimed.

Sherlock calmly replied, "Why that is an excellent suggestion, Watson, and I think our client should continue her fascinating story that I interrupted when I returned. She might even care to explain to you the basis of her awareness of the unicorn, as obvious as it might be to the trained eye."

I was dumbfounded by Sherlock's statement and interrupted before our guest could reply. "Are you going to tell me that you were aware of Miss Leeda's knowledge of the unicorn's presence prior to her mentioning it? Your skills are impressive Sherlock, and at times beyond my comprehension, but how is that possible even for you?"

At that point, the unicorn, enthusiastically interjected, "I can explain that! It is simple. To begin with, being aware of mystical subjects, if she had spent a considerable amount of time excavating crystals in the vicinity of the Scotsman's lochs, then she would have gained an affinity and awareness of a unicorn's presence in the immediate surroundings. We do have a certain aura about us, and if one is deeply attuned to it, that person would easily sense us, even in our invisible phase. It is, what do you call it, quite elementary, Dr. Watson, especially for one skilled in working with *elements* and other minerals. In fact, it should be *crystal* clear!" I groaned at its final comment and even noticed Miss Leeda suppressing a smile.

Sherlock stared directly at the unicorn, slowly responding, "Yes, that about sums up that aspect very nicely. Almost *rock solid*. Now if we can dispense with the clever wordplay, and *ground* this conversation, we will continue. As I came up the stairs, I overheard the start of her explanation, and the rest was obvious. The journal mentioned in both of today's previous cases is hers. As for the timing, there is no such thing as a coincidence. This is all converging very neatly as it should. Now if Miss Leeda would continue telling us her story, we will discover in what new direction this fascinating path will take us."

Daintily retrieving her teacup from the table, she took another sip and continued. "I am somewhat of a contradiction. As a result of more enlightened and knowledgeable parents, I began studying science in general, and more specifically, geology at an early age, while at the same time feeling a connection and oneness to nature and the mystical aspects of Spiritualism. Naturally, I kept my interests in the latter quite secret. One only has to observe the disparity of educational opportunities to realize the disposition towards women who express unconventional ideas. But truthfully, the use of crystals is found in the Bible itself. Twelve specific gemstone crystals are mentioned as being an integral part of Aaron's breastplate, and in the book of Revelations, they are listed as being the foundation of New Jerusalem. So, I continued to quietly study the fascinating metaphysical aspects of crystals along with their geologically scientific properties."

My studies led me to Scotland where I discovered a site containing particularly fascinating fluorite crystals. Fluorite (also known as fluorspar) is the mineral form of calcium fluoride. It is a member of the halide minerals group and crystallizes in an isometric cubic form. It even changes invisible light beyond the violet end of the visible spectrum into blue light. In his 1852 paper, Sir George Stokes described this phenomenon, which he named fluorescence."

"The specific crystals I had found there, were a beautiful purple/green coalescence, quite striking in their appearance. While speaking purely geologically, the only practical purpose for fluorite crystals is in using them as a flux in smelting. However, to one more aligned with the mystical realm, fluorite is a protective and stabilizing stone, used for harmonizing spiritual energy. It increases intuitive abilities and connects the human mind to universal consciousness. To one as focused purely on facts, and as logical as you are, Mr. Holmes, I would not expect you to accept any of this. However, you cannot deny the fact that I pointed out the presence of a unicorn in this room before anyone mentioned it."

Sherlock frowned but did not reply, so she continued. "Fluorite is known to heighten mental abilities, and aid in rapid sorting and processing of information, as well as possessing several other characteristics. But it is not at all known as a healing stone so that you can imagine my surprise, when the longer I stayed and worked in that location, the better I felt. My health was noticeably improving. These particular fluorite specimens were unlike any I had encountered previously, so there had to be something that could explain it. It could be that I had also been bathing regularly in a small loch in the vicinity. Digging up crystals is very strenuous you know, and rather dirty work, so a bath was always most welcome. But it was remarkable how well I felt afterward. I was at a loss to explain the phenomena, when one afternoon while resting near the shoreline, I had dozed off. I awoke suddenly with a sensation of someone, or something watching me. Without moving a muscle, I slowly glanced around till I spotted it, and I could not believe my eyes. A unicorn had stepped out of the brush and after briefly immersing its horn in the water, sipped for a moment, and vanished into the haze. It was truly magnificent, and far beyond my ability to adequately describe, but I will remember that moment, and even more-so the sensation that I felt at that time, forever. That is how I knew there was a unicorn present in this room."

The unicorn, who had been standing next to the table quietly the entire time, nodded its head and interjected, "We can have that effect on people, but only on those truly attuned to us."

Miss Leeda smiled and gazed a moment in the direction of the creature, then went on. "I have routinely recorded each day's activities at the dig site in my journal, so the entire unicorn experience was written down. Having some familiarity with what I have read on the subject of the healing nature of alicorn, I wondered, was it possible that the unicorn had imparted that healing ability to the crystals or the water?

I had selected some samples of the crystals, and the water from the pond to bring back to London to consult with a colleague. I had arrived at King's Cross station, and that is when my backpack was taken. I had just arrived and set it down when a ruffian grabbed it and ran. He quickly disappeared into the crowd, and that was the last I saw of my journal or the crystal specimens. Until today that is."

Then turning to Sherlock, she asked, "How is it that you have copies of those pages? I cannot imagine that a common criminal would see any value in the contents of my backpack, much less, even be able to understand what I was talking about."

Sherlock, resting his head in his hand, pondered a moment, before answering. "I would agree with you on that; the thief was most likely quite disappointed when he discovered what he had taken. He probably took it to the nearest antique and curiosities shop and sold it for whatever he could get. While I do not speculate without a sound foundation, that shop is most likely where Mr. Wilkinson's father found your journal. Being a scholar and scientist, he would have recognized the significance of it. As I mentioned earlier, considering its importance, he had made a copy of it before leaving on his trip which is now looking like an expedition to locate a unicorn."

Stomping its hoof, and snorting, the unicorn added, "Most likely to exploit the healing capabilities of the alicorn. So, humans have not changed at all since Arthur's time."

Miss Leeda, in a gentle voice, replied, "Sadly that may be true for some, but not everyone is of that nature. Your presence, secure and safe, in the study of Sherlock Holmes, the most logical and rational human of this era is proof of that."

Sherlock dismissively responded, "Yes, that may be true, but you have still not explained why you waited to seek my services regarding the theft of your journal, for more than a year after it disappeared. I conducted a brief study and wrote a monologue entitled, *The Significance and Importance of the Length of Time Between the Occurrence of a Theft and the Time it is Reported, and how that Affects the Outcome.* I am curious to see how this instance compares to my conclusions."

With a somewhat bewildered look on her beautiful face, Miss Leeda replied rather skeptically, "Yes, I am sure that might be interesting, but the simple answer is that with no apparent way of retrieving my property, I presumed it lost forever. An opportunity to work on another project came up, and I took it, but my thoughts ever remained with that magical place, and the unicorn. When I just recently finished my new task, I returned to Scotland to continue working on the fluorite dig. Imagine my surprise when I discovered the pond near my excavation area, and the lochs nearby had vanished! I made some inquiries to the local villagers and found out about a scientist and his wife that had recently visited the area asking about unicorns, and healing waters. Then I learned that the owner of the land next door had gone to London to see you about his lochs disappearing. There had to be a connection between my missing journal, the scientist couple showing up, and the disappearance of the pond. I discovered you have quite a reputation, and everyone had spoken so very highly of you. So here I am, a year after the theft."

"Indeed, here you are," Sherlock replied. "While I will not disparage my observational, analytical, or deductive skills, you have Dr. Watson to thank for my reputation, even if he does tend to sensationalize and romanticize what can be explained simply."

"I only write the truth as I observe it, Sherlock," I interjected, "Even if, through your eyes, it appears obviously simple, to others it is more than abstruse, if not altogether incomprehensible."

"That may be, but the answer we are looking for is not to be found in hyperbole." Then turning to the unicorn, he continued. "I take it, the unicorn in Scotland, knows nothing of the whereabouts of the first unicorn."

The creature sighed, "That is true. As I mentioned, all knowledge regarding the whereabouts of the first unicorn ceased to exist in the 1600s. He and his mate vanished as completely as Miss Leeda's crystals."

"Sherlock's expression brightened, and he stood up and stated, "Then all may not be lost. If all goes as I expect, I shall return presently, in 25 minutes, to be precise. Do help yourself to refreshments while I am gone. The flavor of Mrs. Hudson's Earl Grey Cream Tea is literally timeless, I am told."

And with that, he deftly snatched his coat and hat and was once again out the door.

Chapter 8.

PETRUS PLANCIUS.

The Case of the Missing Clocks. (And Sherlock makes a timely observation.)

Sherlock had just left on another mysterious mission, and the unicorn had returned to nibbling on the flatbread muffins, so I took the opportunity to possibly engage in more conversation with the charming Miss Leeda. "Can you tell me more about your experience at the fluorite dig site? Were you not concerned for your safety, working out there all alone by yourself?"

She threw her head back and brightly laughed, with her voice echoing like crystal chimes. "Oh, Dr. Watson, you dear fellow. You need not be concerned for my personal safety. In addition to the sciences, my father also made sure I was adequately trained in other areas as well. I am an expert in pistol, rifle, longbow, and certain Asian martial arts. Not to mention my unique knowledge of botany can be most beneficial."

Taken aback by her comment, I asked, how on earth, mere *plant knowledge* could in anyway be helpful in protecting her.

She smiled cordially and removing a small vial from her handbag, responded. She opened the cork and held it out for me to sniff the aroma. "Now Doctor, tell me what your response is to this botanical mixture." I cautiously sniffed the vial, not knowing what to expect, and found it was quite tantalizing. I sniffed it again to verify, and to be truthful; it was most appetizing. Had it been a meal offering, I would have readily devoured it. "That is incredible. It smells delicious, Miss Leeda." I responded. "Quite tempting, actually."

With a sly smile and a wink, she replied. "Yes, that is the usual response. In the evening at my campsite, I always keep a small pot of stew on the fire with a quantity of this botanical mixture cooked into it. It can render a full grown man unconscious in less than a minute. I assure you, my mere, plant knowledge, has protected me more than once out in the field."

I sat silently for a moment and gazed at her with admiration and awe. She was not only beguiling and alluring, but she was multifaceted as well, with arcane skills in multiple areas. What other fascinating secrets did her coy smile conceal?

Wrinkling its nose, the unicorn piped in, "You do realize, of course, that concoction would never fool a unicorn. Our awareness of the plant world is beyond compare."

She smiled, and replied softly, "Why certainly, but there would be no need to protect myself from a unicorn."

The unicorn reared up and struck a regal yet fearsome pose. "You have obviously not read all of the historical records on unicorns. We can be quite fearsome if provoked."

"That is true," she matter-of-factly, nodded, "but only to those who would harm such an innocent and majestic creature, which I would never do. Not to mention, the fair maiden is often used to lure unicorns into a trap, as they are uncontrollably drawn to us."

She then daintily set her teacup down and gazed out the window. The more I observed and listened to her, the more I felt myself drawn to her. I was about to reply when I heard hurried footsteps on the stairs in the hall. They did not sound like Sherlock's, and my suspicions were confirmed, when a sharp, rapid knocking rang out on the door. The unicorn rapidly faded into invisibility, and Miss Leeda looked at me questioningly.

"Do not be concerned," I mentioned as I arose to answer the door. "it is most likely a prospective client. I will ask whoever it is, to return at a later point in time."

I opened the door and was hurriedly greeted by a frantic looking, tall, slender, gentleman carrying a unique looking cane, and dressed in a brown wool, cutaway morning coat, dark trousers, a paisley vest, and a royal blue ascot. While his attire spoke of upper-class leisure, his manner was anything but relaxed. As soon as I opened the door to request a later meeting, he burst into the room, brushing past me, and gesticulating wildly. With his hands waving back and forth, he spoke rapidly with a slight accent, seemingly without pausing to take a breath. "Good day, Mr. Holmes. I am so glad you are here. There is no time left. I must engage your services."

Noticing Miss Leeda, he turned and addressed her, "Oh, Good day, Ma'am. Please do pardon the intrusion, but this is extremely urgent, and there is just no time left at all."

Then turning back to me, he continued without a break. "How soon can you start, sir? Funds are of no object. I have heard from the most reliable of sources that you are the very best, and I must have your help! No one can help me if you cannot. There is simply no time left. I do not know what I am to do. All is surely lost!"

And with that, he collapsed into the chair across from Miss Leeda and just stared at us, with a wide-eyed, forlorn expression. Somewhat confused myself, I looked back and forth between Miss Leeda, and the odd gentleman, not sure what to do. I did manage to state, "Good day sir, would a cup of tea help to calm you down, or perhaps a nip of brandy? We have some right here. Actually, I am not Sherlock Holmes. My name is Dr. Watson." Then glancing at my watch, I hastily added, "but Sherlock should be back very soon."

Hearing that, he burst from his chair, exclaiming, "Not Sherlock Holmes? Not Sherlock Holmes?? Then all is most assuredly lost. I am out of time! I have failed in the most important task in all of history!" and with that, he fell back into the chair and fainted.

The unicorn materialized and commented, "He is certainly rather overstrung. I would say he is wound tighter than a soprano lute left in the sun for more than a week."

I ignored the creature's comments and was reaching towards my medical bag to retrieve the smelling salts, when Miss Leeda quickly pulled another vial from her handbag and removing the stopper, slowly wafted it under his nose. He coughed, opened his eyes, blinked several times, shook his head, and frantically exclaimed. "Quickly, what time is it?"

Then, looking even more astonished, and pointing directly at the unicorn, who had not yet phased back to invisibility, his eyes grew wide, and he cried out, "Wait! Perhaps, I am not too late, Is it you? Are you really here? Have you somehow returned? But it's not possible! How could it be? I still don't have the missing clocks!" Then looking back at me he implored, "Tell me how it is possible!"

I shrugged my shoulders, as I was at a loss for words. It appeared as if he somehow, had recognized the unicorn, as unlikely as that seemed, and he was quite confident that the mysterious and urgent task he was referring to, was the most important in history. It was unimaginable as to what it might have been. Miss Leeda closed her vial and returned it to her handbag. I could not help but wonder what other botanical curiosities were hidden deep within in its velvet folds.

My curiosity would have to wait, however, as just then, the door opened, and Sherlock returned with a ragged, dusty, backpack held in one hand. Handing it to Miss Leeda, he addressed us all collectively, not showing any surprise or concern regarding the additional gentleman in the room.

"I do believe that these are the missing crystals in question. Yes, I am fully aware that it is prodigious, after all this time that I should locate them. I assure you it was quite elementary; just a matter of recalling the nearest antiquities and oddities shop, to King's Cross Station, which conveniently, was not far away. Fortunately, I recently completed a monograph; *A Comprehensive list of all the Antiquities, Oddities, Curiosities, Collectibles, Pawn, and Second-hand shops in London, cross-referenced by their Proximity to Train Stations, and other Public Places where Certain less than Desirable Aspects of Society, who may have Illicitly Acquired an item of Value, and want to Dispose of it Quickly.* Knowing that the ruffian, who pinched Miss Leeda's bag, would be anxious to dispose of it, which he was, and the lack of monetary value to the untrained eye, I determined that it would most likely still be there, which it was. I also concluded that a buyer of such items would be pleased to be rid of it, which he was, and as such, I would be able to retrieve it, which I was. Hence, here it is, which resolves your case, Ma'am."

Then turning to the beleaguered and frantic gentlemen sitting on the chair, he addressed him, "Now let us proceed directly to your case. I am Sherlock Holmes. You, sir, are from Holland, and a member of an ancient, secret society dedicated to certain aspects of astronomy and horology. Your appearance here is to engage my services regarding your missing clocks, which also explains your astonishment at the presence of a unicorn, whom you somewhat recognized, but were not expecting. Am I correct?"

The gentleman's eyes grew wide with astonishment and acknowledgement, and I must confess, although I have witnessed firsthand, countless demonstrations of Sherlock's uncanny deductive skills, I was impressed as well.

The gentleman was incredulous and stammered. "But how can you possibly know all of that? You just walked into this room! I have heard you are the best, but this is simply unfathomable."

Sherlock casually gazed at the ceiling, taking delight, in the perplexed astonishment of the mysterious gentleman, and then answered. "It is more than simple, my good man but only for one who truly observes. I overheard your comments as I came up the stairs and judging by your accent, I can tell you are from Holland. Firstly, the unique ring on your finger, and secondly, your lapel pin, point to membership in a secret society. The finer details of your pin connect you to both horology, by the outer clock face on its perimeter, and to astronomy, by the depiction of the constellation, Monoceros, on its interior. The small telescope rather cleverly built into your cane, by the way, also tells me of your connection to astronomy. Your mistaken recognition of the present unicorn somehow connects you to my current task in determining the whereabouts of the first unicorn. That also explains your appearance here, to engage my services regarding your missing clocks, which may, in fact, provide the answer which we are all seeking. So, you see, it is really, quite simple."

Chapter 9.

While Seconds are Ticking Away, (Literally) we take a Moment, to get Caught up on over 200 years of History. (But, only the unwritten, and esoteric aspects that pertained to our circumstances.)

A hushed silence briefly fell over the room when Sherlock finished speaking, and then chaos erupted, as everyone, including the unicorn, started talking at once.

"Mr. Holmes, thank you ever so much for locating and recovering my crystals. After all this time, it is truly wonderful! How do you do it?" Miss Leeda inquired of Sherlock.

Pointing its alicorn directly at the quivering gentleman, the unicorn slowly articulated a question which in truth, was actually more of a demand, "Tell me, sir. Exactly what do you know of the first unicorn? What can you tell me of his whereabouts?"

Then apparently, regaining its composure, it added in the gentlest of voices, "I assure you, sir, any information would be most welcomed and appreciated. Since the 1600s, all knowledge of him and his mate have been as impossible to discern as a pixy's shadow in the fading light of a winter solstice crescent moon."

The mysterious gentleman, also calming down for the first time since his arrival, surprised everyone there, by responding, "Yes, you are quite right, those are indeed the most difficult conditions in which to perceive the shadow of a pixy. Nearly as difficult as capturing the breath of a dragon. Please don't ask me how I know... "

Sherlock then interrupted, pointing out, "I am sure that would make a fascinating discussion, and your comparison of allegories and metaphors is quite intriguing, but as you previously pointed out, there is apparently little time left for you to complete your task, so I suggest you apprise us of its details."

With a startled look on his face, he looked askance, and replied, "Yes, you are quite right. There is little time left. I must eschew the distractions. I shall tell you all. My name is Brecht Van der Lucht, but that is not important. What is important, is my task. You are correct, Mr. Holmes. I am a member of a secret society that has existed since the 1600s. The same time that the first unicorn disappeared. In fact, it was our organization that facilitated the disappearance of the creature and its mate."

When he said that, I could see the emotion building in the eyes of the unicorn, but it remained motionless and listened as Mr. Van der Lucht went on with his strange tale.

"At that time in history, the persecution of unicorns, and the hunt for their alicorns had become so prevalent and pervasive, that unless something were done, unicorns might have been hunted to extinction. I cannot imagine a world in which such a creature does not exist. It would be a loss to all humanity. Fortunately, there was a group of individuals; scientists, poets, and philosophers they were, who felt as I do now and who resolved to do something about the situation before it was too late. They formed a secret organization to protect the first unicorn through the ages. That is the group to which I belong, the Planciuns, named after Petrus Plancius, the Dutch astronomer, cartographer, and clergyman.

"They conferred with the creature and its mate and tried to determine a place where they could hide the unicorns where no one could possibly find them, and they would be safe from the hunters. That is when the unicorn revealed its ability to 'shift phases.' It was described as a way in which the creature changed its appearance, which explains all of the different descriptions of unicorns over the ages."

The unicorn, standing across from him, nodded in agreement, and pointed out that it too had mentioned that bit of information. Mr. Van der Lucht also nodded his head and pressed on.

"But in spite of its shapeshifting ability, it always retained some semblance of the appearance of the creature known throughout time as a unicorn. It could not hide its basic physical or spiritual nature. 'But what if they could?' asked one of our members who dabbled in alchemy, astronomy, and other arcane arts. 'What if the spirits of the first unicorn and its mate could be transformed into some entity or form that could hide them until it was safe to return.' That was the solution! Our society had only to discover a way to bring it about. They spent almost a year working with the creatures to determine the process, and they finally succeeded. There were several close calls when hunters almost discovered the unicorns, but they survived to undergo the transformation. This may sound implausible in light of today's scientific knowledge, but our organization discovered a way to transfer the creature's spirits or essence to a place in the heavens."

At that point, both Sherlock and the unicorn exclaimed, "The constellation Monoceros!"

Mr. Van der Lucht slowly nodded in agreement. "Yes, Monoceros is a faint constellation on the celestial equator. Its name is Greek for unicorn. Its discovery is attributed to our namesake, Petrus Plancius, who in 1612, first included it on a celestial globe. But unknown to the rest of the world, is that he was also a part of its very creation. The creatures are still up there now. No trace of them has been seen or felt in our world since that time. But due to the mechanics of the procedure, there was a time limit that was part of the transformation. For them to be able to return to Earth, the process must be reversed by a specific time and date, or they will be lost forever. That was the sole purpose of our society, and my life, to pass down through the ages, the secret of the process, and to protect the apparatus required to perform it until the designated time, but I have failed, and so close to the fulfillment of our legacy!"

He then stopped speaking and stared down at the floor in defeat.

Sherlock looked first at the unicorn, and then at the gentleman and calmly asked, "Mr. Van der Lucht, what is the deadline for the reversal of the process? What are the time and date?"

He nervously replied. "It is midnight, tonight. We have mere hours from now, and the clocks required to reverse the process have been purloined. Yesterday, someone made off with them. They have always been kept securely under lock and key, but they are missing, and unless they are recovered by midnight, the first unicorn and his mate will be gone forever!"

Chapter 10.

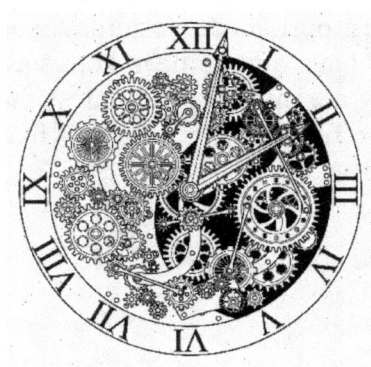

We Return to The Case of the Missing Clocks. (And it is somewhat like a hungry clock that goes back four seconds.)

The unicorn said nothing, and simply stamped its hoof, while Miss Leeda, with a look of concern, implored, "That is terrible! Is there anything at all we can do? I would be willing to help in any way possible."

I interjected, "We must be able to do something! Can the special clocks required for the procedure be recreated in any way?"

Van der Lucht shook his head negatively and sighed. "No, that would be impossible. Their maker took the secret of their design to his grave. The construction of the two clocks was an extremely complex achievement back then. I assure you, there is no one alive today, who could repeat the task."

"Then it is elementary," Sherlock stated. "We must locate the timepieces before the deadline. Now tell me everything you know about the clocks, where they were kept, who may have known about them, how they were secured, and in particular, every detail you can remember about the day they disappeared."

Mr. Van der Lucht sighed and began, "Pieter Van den Keere is remembered as a Dutch engraver, publisher and globe maker, but what is not known is that he also dabbled in horology or clock-making. His most significant contribution, which will never be known to the world, was his construction of the two clocks that were used to facilitate the first unicorn's transformation. It was Petrus Plancius who discovered the process, but it was Van den Keere who created the clockwork mechanism that made it function. He incorporated several crystals in his design of the apparatus. It was based on the knowledge that all creatures have an energy or *spirit* if you will, that dwells within their physical bodies. The actual process involved the phase transformation abilities of the unicorns, the piezoelectric energy of the crystals, the temporal characteristics of the clocks, knowledge of the celestial sphere, and I am sure, several additional factors that were never fully explained.

"The inner circle of our group consisted of the Uranographers or celestial cartographers. Uranography combines astronomy and cartography and consists of mapping stars, galaxies, and other astronomical objects on the celestial sphere. The result of their efforts was that the spirits of the creatures were transferred from their Earthly physical bodies into the heavens.

"While all of this was done in utmost secrecy, Van den Keere's wife, Anna Beurt, somehow did find out about the unicorns. It was said that she was altogether enraptured by them and was utterly devastated when they became the constellation. She was never the same afterward. It is not known what became of her, but some records that indicate Van Den Keere remarried in 1623. I do not know if it is of importance, but it was rumored that Anna's final words to him were, 'You will be sorry. They will never return to you!' I do not know what she may have meant. It was thoroughly understood by all the members of the group at the time that the unicorns would not be returning until the far distant future."

Sherlock gazed silently into the distance and then commented. "Indeed, what did she mean? I wonder... Now tell me about where the clocks to be used for their return were kept."

"That is simple; they were right here in London. The society has maintained a two-room flat on Gloucester Place near Dorset Street, not far from here actually. While our organization began in the Netherlands in 1612, the keepers of the clocks and the secret process to return the Unicorns moved to England a century ago. Membership in the society has always been very select and follows the Dutch lineage of those who comprised the original group. In order to keep our group alive and prevent an untimely end to it, there have always been two keepers. In case one should die unexpectedly, the organization would still go on. My counterpart has been making inquiries and perusing shoppes where items, such as old clocks, might have been sold, but so far he has not found any leads."

Looking at Miss Leeda and then Sherlock, he added, "I only hope that you can find the clocks as quickly as you did her crystals. We have maintained a residence in our building for decades. The room where the chronographs were kept was an interior room, with no windows, and no outside access. In addition, they have been held in a secure safe all these years. At least we thought it was secure.

"The only other person who knew anything about our organization and its purpose, is my associate keeper, Hendrick Van de Berg, a person of impeccable character, and as dedicated to our cause as I am. He is a quiet man, who spends his time reading, stargazing, and maintaining the more ordinary timepieces we keep in the flat. It is a tradition that keepers of the clocks lead a reserved life to avoid drawing attention to our purpose. Our organization is funded by an endowment that pays all of our expenses, so money has never been a problem. We simply make withdrawals as needed. I cannot fathom how anyone could have discerned our presence and purpose. Nothing else was taken from the room, and there were many other items more valuable than those two clocks. To the untrained eye, the unicorn clocks were ornate and unique, but not expensive looking, if you understand."

He then removed from his inside jacket pocket, a tattered photograph of two rather strange looking clocks and showed them to us.

Sherlock nodded and commented, "Yes. From your description, it appears that the person who took them knew exactly what they were after and was well-prepared for any obstacles that may have been in the way. Gloucester Place is not far from here. I would like to examine your residence. Has anything been disturbed since the theft? Has Scotland Yard been notified?"

"No to both of your questions. We try to keep a low profile, so I thought it would be best to consult you directly. We did visit a few of the antique shops to see if they turned up, but it was to no avail. Yesterday, the day of the theft, there was a problem with the fireplace, so we called in a chimney sweep to tend to it. Before he arrived, we locked the inner room, and then waited outside while he took care of his task. When he was done, he called us back in to demonstrate that it was working again and that nothing was amiss with the contents of the room. The interior door was still locked, so we did not suspect foul play. It was apparent that he did not carry anything but his tools as he left. Yet, today, when we entered the clock room, we discovered the theft. I came straight away to see you, while my associate is checking the local shoppes. The chimney sweep looked like any other sweep in London, rather small and diminutive in stature, facial features obscured by soot and dirt. He disappeared into the street when he was done. That is about all I can tell you."

Holmes pondered momentarily and replied, "Yes, a perfect operation. The sweep most likely had an accomplice waiting on the roof, and that is how the clocks might have been removed, by lifting them up through the chimney."

At that point, I suggested that the thief and his accomplice could have caused the chimney problem itself. The entire operation was probably planned and set up well in advance.

"Watson," Sherlock replied, you know I do not jump to conclusions, but in this case, you may be right. Judging by the photo, they are not very large and would fit up through the chimney. Yes. Let us investigate the premises to see if they left anything that could lead us to them."

The unicorn immediately asked, "May I be of assistance? My perception is beyond measure."

"And I am very attuned to crystals," Added Miss Leeda, "if the clocks are perchance still on the premises, I could sense the crystals."

"That may be the case." said Sherlock, "but I would prefer first to investigate the premises myself, so nothing is inadvertently disturbed. As the unicorn can render itself invisible, you may both accompany us if you do not mind waiting outside while I initially inspect the rooms. Perhaps we may find something which both of your particular skills can further explain."

And with that, we left the building, with no idea what a strange turn of events was waiting for us.

Chapter 11.

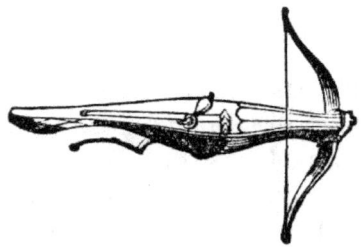

A Strange Turn of Events. (And we discover that not only, does time fly like an arrow, but sometimes, arrows fly almost all the time.)

The keeper's flat on Gloucester Place was a short distance away, and it did not take us long to get there. We walked quickly through the brisk London haze, saying nothing along the way. My thoughts wandered between the lovely Miss Leeda, possibly getting to know her better, and what new evidence Sherlock might uncover when we arrived. I was confident that his sharply tuned observational skills would reveal something significant.

Van der Lucht, who was leading the way, stopped in front of a drab, unimposing brownstone building. It was normal looking in every way and gave no impression of the many secrets it had hidden over the previous decades. Miss Leeda and I waited nearby while Sherlock carefully studied the building, looking at it from different angles.

He paused and asked where, *exactly*, the particular chimney sweep Van der Lucht had engaged, had been standing, when he came out to locate and hire one and was informed that the sweep had been casually leaning against the stair railings, looking for all the world, like he was just taking a short break. Van der Lucht had been pleased to locate one so quickly and had not considered it unusual. Sherlock examined the area meticulously, taking specific note of a one spot, and then went up the stairs into the building with the keeper.

While he was gone, I took the opportunity, and made casual conversation with Miss Leeda for a while, eventually asking her what she thought of the building, and if she had noticed anything of interest.

She lightly laughed, and replied, "That depends on how you define, 'of interest,' now doesn't it? If you notice, their building has just the one flat, but there are adjoining buildings on each side of it. Do not look at the one to the left, but someone has been observing us from that window since we arrived. And the moment Mr. Holmes and Mr. Van der Lucht went inside, the person watching from the window on the right, suddenly vanished."

I restrained myself and did not look at either building, but looked directly at her and asked, "Don't you think we should go inside and let them know? They could be in some type of danger."

"I think not, Dr. Watson, no real harm has come to the clock keepers all this time. Only the clocks themselves have been taken."

"Yes, but now, they have made their move," I insisted, "whatever it is, so it could be that they will be bolder and ready to do whatever may be necessary to stop anyone from interfering."

She demurely coughed into a delicate lace handkerchief, and replied, "That may be quite true Dr. Watson. In fact, you should bend down to adjust your shoelace, NOW!"

Without thinking, I quickly stooped towards my shoe, and a small arrow-like dart flew past me, just missing my neck. It struck the ground, and I turned and saw the curtains of the window on the left fluttering, but no one was visible. I removed my handkerchief, carefully picked up the dart, and asked her, "Now would you consider going inside to inform Sherlock?"

She quickly agreed, and looking both directions for any additional darts, we made our way up the cobblestone walkway and stairs. As we did, I was sure I heard the whistle of additional tiny arrows flying past us.

We entered the hallway of the flat and paused a moment to determine where Sherlock might be investigating. Hearing nothing, I poked my head into the apartment and saw him standing very still in front of the fireplace staring at the fire-box. Without turning or looking in our direction, he offhandedly addressed us. "Do come in Watson, Miss Leeda, I have already determined everything that has happened here, and while it was very straightforward, I feel there is a great deal more going on here than we were led to believe, and it may not be safe to remain in the hallway. Do come in and close the door."

At that moment I felt Miss Leeda brush by me as she hurried into the flat, pulling me with her, while yet another small arrow flew past as the door was slammed shut.

"What exactly is going on here?" I exclaimed for the second time that day.

Sherlock turned to face us and stated. "It is obvious; there is a second secret group or society involved, and they have been observing the keepers for a long time. They have agents in the apartment's adjoining buildings, on both sides, and have been monitoring this particular flat quite closely. The chimney sweep that just happened to be outside their door when the keepers had the problem with their fireplace was one of the organization's agents and a female at that. She did indeed send the clocks up to an accomplice on the roof via the chimney, scratching the top of the fire-box along the way. While they are serious regarding their intent, they are not killers, as the small arrows they have been firing, are not poisonous, just treated with a substance that would render the victim unconscious for a period."

As he finished speaking, he motioned towards a finely carved, rosewood slipper chair, in which Van der Lucht was slumped over asleep.

"We had just made it into the hallway when several darts were fired through the open window on the back wall. I got him safely inside on onto the chair. Determining what substance, they used on the point of the dart was child's play for me. He should be awake soon. So, should the unconscious lady, you will find securely bound to a chair, in the clock room. I surprised her when I entered and was easily able to subdue her. She should be able to answer several questions about what is really going on here."

Miss Leeda stepped over to the clock room door, curiously looked in and then rapidly turned back with a look of alarm, crying out! "She's gone!"

We all three quickly entered the clock room, and not far from a large safe, found an empty armchair in the center of the room. On the floor around the chair were the remains of the cord Sherlock had used to secure her.

"Well, this is an interesting turn of events." Sherlock nonchalantly stated.

Chapter 12.

Sherlock Appears to be Stumped. (But only momentarily, and it was a safe bet, that I would have never guessed the solution, or where it led to.)

"This *is* an interesting turn of events," Sherlock stated again, as he glanced around the room.

"How *did* she manage to do that?" I heard him mutter under his breath, sounding rather stumped. Then he addressed us. "If you please, if you could both look in on our host, Mr. Van der Lucht, whilst I determine what became of our elusive guest. That would be appreciated. I will need the room empty to concentrate. Do make sure the rest of the windows are closed. We would not want any more arrows finding their way in."

Somewhat bewildered, Miss Leeda and I returned to the main sitting room. It was well appointed, with stained glass lamps, a brown leather couch, and a large desk, in addition to the chair in which the keeper was unconsciously slumped over. On both sides of the offending fireplace, the walls entertained built-in bookshelves which were full of many ancient looking volumes and tomes, as well as several old and ornate timepieces, and other devices.

Miss Leeda had retrieved a glass of water from the adjoining kitchen, commenting, "The kitchen window is closed and secure. Have you checked the bedrooms? They could be another avenue of access for those pesky arrows. We would not want to make it easier for whoever is behind this."

I was most impressed by her calm manner, and ability to take everything in stride, somewhat like a sea captain ploughing steadfastly through a raging storm. As I went and checked the bedroom windows, I found myself thinking back to her description of the geological digs and being utterly alone for days on end out in the wilderness. She was in truth, quite indefatigable.

"They are secure," I answered. Then my thoughts turned to Sherlock in the clock room. How could an unconscious lady, securely tied to a chair, have simply vanished? It did not seem possible, but there had to be an explanation. I certainly could not fathom it, however, in my defense, I had not gotten a very good look at the room.

"He is coming around." Miss Leeda stated.

I turned and saw our host, Van der Lucht regaining consciousness, and being offered the water she had brought in. He leaned his head back for a moment, took a few deep breaths, looked down again, and slowly drank the water. "Thank you… what happened? How did I get in this chair? It is all somewhat unclear."

"You were hit with a tranquilizer dart. "I stated. "Apparently, there are adversaries in the buildings on both sides of your flat. Sherlock is in the clock room now, determining how exactly one of them managed to vanish when she was tied to a chair."

"What? There was an intruder in the clock room? And she escaped?"

He cried as he suddenly attempted to stand up, only to weakly fall back into the chair. Miss Leeda endeavored to calm him, assuring him that Sherlock would undoubtedly determine what had occurred. "We are safe for now, and from what I have seen, Mr. Holmes has everything well under control."

She was about to go into greater detail, when Sherlock reentered the room speaking rather loudly, as he held up a hastily scribbled note, apparently for the unicorn, still in its immaterial state, to read. "Well, I would say your intruder has most certainly escaped. There is no trace of her in the clock room, whatsoever. She has outwitted us all. If you are feeling well enough Mr. Van der Lucht, I would suggest that we return to Baker Street, there are some items that I would like to discuss with you, and this may not be the most secure location. I think we should leave immediately. Do be careful now!"

And with that, he ushered us out of the room, making sure he loudly slammed the door, securing it behind us. He did not say a word as we wound our way through the wintery grey streets of London and returned to our flat in Baker Street. It was not until our door was closed, did he explain, just what exactly, was going on.

"Well, if my calculations are correct, we should soon have some real answers courtesy of our unicorn's unique ability. It was obvious to me that there was no way the intruder could have left the room, even if she were able to somehow escape from the rope that secured her to the chair, so I knew she had to still be in the clock room. The only place she could have hidden was inside the safe. She was rather diminutive, and it was more than large enough for someone of her size, as the clocks that had been stored inside had been removed. If I could make her think that we had not found her and left, then she would come out of her hiding place and return to the organization that she is a part of...,"

"And the unicorn, in its invisible state, should be able to follow her, directly to the group. That is brilliant Holmes!" I exclaimed.

"But if this organization is also well aware of unicorns, and their abilities, which they seem to be, wouldn't they know about the creature's phase transformation skills, and ability to become invisible?" asked Miss Leeda.

"That may be," stated Sherlock, "but that information is immaterial if she were unaware of the unicorn's presence, to begin with. It had fortuitously remained in its transparent state the entire time we were there, and we made no clear reference at all to its presence. I was able to scribble a written note with my plan, and quickly show it to the unicorn before anyone could have noticed. When it returns, we should get some useful information pertaining to this second organization."

"But how would you have known that it had entered the room and was present if it had been invisible the entire time?" I asked. "What if it was still waiting outside? Then what?"

Sherlock waved his hand dismissively and replied. "It is all part of proper observation and detection, Watson. You obviously had not noticed the plate of flatbread muffins that was on the table in the sitting room when we arrived but had somehow vanished before you left. There is only one creature that could have accomplished that with no one but me discerning their disappearance. The unicorn does seem to have a particular affinity for flatbread muffins."

"That is because they are so uniquely flavorful, and they have not yet been invented in the time of King Arthur," came the voice of the unicorn, still in its immaterial state.

"There is nothing at all like them in my time period. I really must bring some back with me when this adventure is brought to a successful conclusion. Perchance, I may even consider bringing back the recipe, unless, of course, that would change history in some obscure way; beyond your already having introduced King Arthur to tea several hundred years prior to its existence that is. Not to mention your plan which caused the creation of fraudulent bodies of the king and queen of Camelot…"

"Enough talk about tea and biscuits and bodies, if you please," answered Sherlock, "what did you discover regarding the intruder? Where did she go when she emerged from the safe?"

"Well, that is the interesting part." The unicorn stated as it transitioned back to solid form. "She is actually right here with me."

And much to all of our surprise, there she was astride the unicorn!

Chapter 13.

History is Truth. Don't be Misled by the Facts. (Meaning, we get to hear the same 200 years of history again, but this time, from a very different point of view.)

"Please, do not be alarmed!" She cried out. "I mean you no harm. In truth, I am here to help. I can explain everything if you will just let me!"

The unicorn nodded its head affirmatively, adding, "I believe we should trust her, Wizard Holmes. Listen to what she has to say. It is most fascinating."

"This *is* an interesting turn of events," Sherlock commented, as he observed the newcomer while she dismounted from the unicorn and brushed off her tattered, and soot-covered outfit. It was apparently intended to give her the appearance of a young man. It seemed most likely that she was the chimney sweep that had previously plundered the clocks. Why she would have returned to the scene of the crime, was beyond me. When she removed the somewhat oversized, wool newsboy hat, which had obscured most of her facial features, her long blond hair tumbled down her shoulders, and it was evident that she was in her early twenties. I wondered what had caused her apparent change of allegiance if she indeed did intend to help us, as she had stated.

My thoughts, however, were interrupted by both, Miss Leeda, and Mr. Van Der Lucht, who suddenly stood up, pointed at her, and cried out, "You!" almost in unison.

Sherlock then raised both his hands, palms outward, in a pacifying gesture to settle them down, calmly stating, "Yes, indeed. It is obvious that this is not only the chimney sweep that you, Mr. Van der Lucht, hired the day the clocks were stolen, but also the very same thief who ran off with your backpack a year ago, Miss Leeda. I am certain that young Iris here, (That is your name, is it not?) can explain everything. Her change of heart towards her former comrades will be most beneficial to us. We will now have, so to speak, ears and eyes in the enemy camp."

This time all of us in the room including the newcomer, evidentially named Iris, looked at Sherlock in surprise and asked how on Earth he could have known that.

"It is all in the subtle, nearly invisible physical signs a person gives when making a statement. If you watch someone close enough and know exactly what to look for, you can tell almost anything about almost anyone. My personal experience in observing the criminal element, as well as their victims, has provided a wealth of opportunities for me to observe winks and blinks, twitches and tics, shudders and shivers, flutters and flickers, and a multitude of other even less visible fluctuations in a person's demeanor when they are speaking. They all add up to clearly indicate, whether or not they are telling the truth. Not to mention a good deal about their personal background. It is all collected in a paper I wrote on the subject, titled *Seeing is Believing, but not all of the Time, Depending on Significant but Unseen Facial and Body Movements, Typically Missed by the Unobservant.*" I am still working on the title.""

Then Sherlock turned and stared directly and intently at the young lady and continued. "For example, Iris here is an orphan, who took to robbery at a young age to survive. After her theft of Miss Leeda's backpack, she was then recruited by the organization that stole the clocks. She obviously experienced a change of heart when she finally found herself in the presence of a genuine unicorn. Am I correct so far Miss Iris?"

Iris stood wide-eyed and silent for only a moment before exclaiming, "How could you know any of that just by looking at me? And how is it even possible that you could know my name when we have never met?"

"Yes, Sherlock," I interjected, even knowing you as well as I do, I cannot fathom how you pulled off that one. There has to be more to it than that."

Holmes coughed, looked at me, and replied, "Well, as you know, Watson, accurate observation and truly seeing the unseen is vitally important, but it also helps if, given the opportunity, you ask the right questions at the right time. For example, when I retrieved Miss Leeda's backpack from the pawn shop, I asked the proprietor if he could tell me all that he knew about the person he had purchased it from. An extra quid helped loosen his tongue quite nicely. That is actually how I knew her name, orphan status, and criminal background, but her change of heart and sincerity I deduced by my exceptionally keen and highly refined observational skills."

Then turning back to the newcomer, he addressed her. "Now, Miss Iris, why don't you tell us your story? You are among friends."

She glanced at us all, stared long and intently at the unicorn, sighed and began. "As Mr. Holmes stated, my name is Iris, and I was orphaned at an early age, although I was educated before my parents died and left me with nothing. I did what I needed to do, in order to survive. My small stature allowed me to get in and out of tight spaces, which was useful, both as an honest chimney sweep, and in less than honest endeavors as well. When I stole your backpack a year ago, I did look through the contents, and your journal, before I sold it to the curiosity shop. It was quite interesting and introduced me to the wonder of unicorns. I was intrigued, and fascinated, and started seeking more information on the subject. That is when I came across the other organization.

"Their group has no real name, but they have been in existence as long as Mr. Van der Lucht's society, the Planciuns. The wife of Mr. Van den Keere, Anna Beurt, started the organization. She was truly captivated and mesmerized by the creatures and was so devastated by the departure of the first unicorn and its mate that she vowed they would never return. To that end, she collected a group of people to make certain that it would not happen. Of course, her stated goal was to protect the unicorns and keep them safe in their place of refuge, but in truth, it was to ensure that they never returned to Earth. In a similar method as the Planciuns, she recruited like-minded individuals over the years to keep the organization and its purpose alive. They have been observing and monitoring the Planciuns since the 1600s and waiting for the opportunity to seize the apparatus that could bring the creatures back."

At that point, the unicorn interjected. "I do not blame her actually. When you have been touched by, or even just been in the presence of the most magnificent creature ever to walk the face of the Earth, you will never be the same. Most individuals who encounter one, do benefit from the experience, and it changes their life for the better. But some, like Anna Beurt, react negatively, with feelings of remorse, regret, or even anger that the experience was so fleeting and brief. Those are the ones that many times became unicorn hunters. But to seek to keep them from ever returning is very sad."

Continuing her story, Miss Iris went on. "I became involved in Anna's organization, because at first, I did think they wanted to protect the unicorns, and keep them safe, but it was only, after I had taken the clocks, that I realized that their one desire was to prevent the creatures from ever returning. In addition, when the group learned of the existence of another unicorn living in Scotland, they determined to use the clocks to send it to the Monoceros constellation as well. They sent me back to Mr. Van der Lucht's flat to locate the process. That is when all of you arrived."

She then turned and gazed intently at the unicorn, continuing, "And that is when I sensed *your* presence. I felt something that I had never in my life experienced. I wondered aloud what could it be, and when you materialized and spoke to me, I was overwhelmed. I knew, from that point on, I could no longer support Anna's organization. I had to return here with you. Can you ever forgive me for being a part of them?"

The unicorn was about to reply when Sherlock interrupted. "Yes, yes. That is all wonderful; I am sure the unicorn understands and forgives, but right now, we must react quickly and recover the clocks so that the process can be reversed before the deadline."

Looking at his pocket watch, he asked, "What can you tell us about where they are located? Do you know how many they have guarding them? And most importantly, how we might get them back?"

Miss Iris looked away, coughed, and stammered for a moment before replying, and then finally blurted out. "Well, that may be a bit difficult. They have a dragon guarding them."

Chapter 14.

Nothing Complicates things like a Dragon in the Way of your Objective. (Especially one with a grudge.)

At that point, everyone in the room except the unicorn responded to Miss Iris's statement almost simultaneously. "Did you say a dragon? Here? Impossible!" exclaimed Van der Lucht.

"Really? A genuine dragon? Fire breathing and all? How fascinating. This is becoming most interesting," commented Miss Leeda.

Sherlock merely nodded, and said, "A dragon. Indeed. Why am I not surprised?"

I, myself, was not looking forward to another encounter with a dragon, even if our last one went relatively well, and simply muttered, "Not again."

The unicorn, however, was silent until everyone had spoken, and then stated, "Yes, That's it. It has to be

Tourmaline the Terrible. It makes perfect sense. That would explain a great deal. The only thing worse than an unfriendly dragon is one with a grudge, or maybe a toothache, you have *no* idea how bad they can be when they have a toothache."

"But Tourmaline is just a crystalline boron silicate mineral compounded with other elements," Miss Leeda interrupted. "It is a semi-precious gemstone. What has that to do with dragons? Friendly or otherwise? With or without a toothache?"

The unicorn shook its head negatively responding. "Tourmaline the Terrible is its name. All dragons take their first name from a crystal or mineral that describes their color and scales, and their surname is based on their temperament. You will recall, the dragon we encountered during our adventure in Camelot, was called Malachite the Musical, for his vibrant green scales, and for his love of music and musical instruments."

Mr. Van der Lucht nervously replied. "I think I understand. I prefer *The Musical* much better than *The Terrible.* Why exactly is he called that?"

"And what color are his scales?" Asked Miss Leeda, adding, "The mineral tourmaline is found in a variety of different colors. Usually, iron-rich tourmalines are black to deep brown, while magnesium-rich varieties are brown to yellow, and lithium-rich tourmalines are almost any color of the spectrum."

"Well, that is part of the problem." The unicorn stated. "All of Tourmaline the Terrible's family had radiant red, green, blue, yellow, or deep black scales, and were very much admired by their fellow dragons. His scales, however, were colorless; a rather drab, cream-grey shade of no specific color at all. It is rather embarrassing in the world of dragons. That left him quite ill-tempered, to begin with. One could hardly look in his direction without him tearing a tree out of the ground in anger. To make up for his lack of physical appearance, he excelled in chess. He poured his entire being into the game and was respected as the best chess player in the entire Mystical Realm. That is until he lost a match to the first unicorn. He has held a grudge since that time. He vowed he would get his revenge somehow, and that he would regain his champion status. No one gave it much thought until the first unicorn and his mate disappeared in the 1600s, and Tourmaline was again the reigning champion. It stands to reason that he would not want the unicorns to return, though how he became associated with Anna's group, I really do not know. Mystical creatures typically tend to avoid humans."

"A fascinating story," Sherlock stated enthusiastically. "Now we have something to move forward with. All we need to do is locate this dragon, get him to agree to a game of chess, place a small wager, such as handing over the clocks, on the outcome of the game, defeat him, and recover the clocks. Elementary!"

The unicorn looked at Holmes questionably and declared. "You do realize that this is the reigning chess champion of the Mystical Realm for more than the last two hundred years that we are talking about. And you do not want to know what happens to those who lose a championship match to him."

I thought back to our previous adventure and Sherlock's victorious encounter with Malachite the Musical and realized that the outcome of losing that challenge had never indeed been explicitly stated. I decided that in truth, I did not want to know, and was quite glad that Sherlock had been successful.

Miss Iris quietly said, "I do know where the dragon and the clocks are, and I can lead you there if you really think that this is the best approach. But I must warn you; I have seen the dragon. Not up close, mind you, only from a distance. A rather far distance and that was close enough. You might consider something simpler and less dangerous like flying a hot air balloon up to the constellation Monoceros, to bring back the Unicorns. Or perhaps flying to Mars, or maybe visiting the inside of an active volcano. Any of those might be considerably safer than confronting the dragon."

Sherlock waved his hand dismissively and replied, "Well, everyone knows that a hot air balloon could never make a journey that far, and since, in the last several days, I have already been to the planet Mars, and to the inside of an active volcano, and survived both of those experiences, our only choice left is to confront the dragon. Now tell me more about where they are and how to get there."

"But what could you possibly have to wager, that a dragon would be willing to risk losing the clocks?" Inquired Van der Lucht. "If I understand correctly he knows that without the clocks, the first unicorn can never return. What could possibly cause him to consider risking that?"

Sherlock turned and looked towards Miss Leeda and replied. "Actually, it was something *you* said about the chemical composition of Tourmaline crystals, and the variety of colors the mineral occurs in; that and the result of a few of my own recent chemical experiments."

"Do you mean that foul smelling incident that left the multicolored stains on the wall over there, just from the vapors?" I asked.

"Exactly!" Sherlock replied with a wide grin.

Miss Leeda stood up and walked over to the wall, and examined the stains, sniffed them, turned to Sherlock and said, "Lithium." Then she smiled and said, "I think I understand where you are going with this. Yes, it could work. You appeal to Tourmaline's vanity. But we would need a considerable amount of the substance for a creature the size of a dragon. Fortunately, I am well-acquainted with Dr. Augustus Matthiessen, the chemist, and physicist who co-developed the process for isolating lithium in 1855. I do believe he would cooperate."

"Wonderful!" replied Sherlock, enthusiastically, "Then it is a plan."

Utterly bewildered, I interrupted and asked, "Could someone please tell me what you two are talking about?"

Sherlock sighed and explained, "It is the Lithium, my dear, obtuse friend. You are a doctor. You, more than anyone here, should understand how deficiencies in certain substances can affect one's condition or appearance. If we provide a significant amount of Lithium for the dragon to ingest, the mineral should alter the color of his scales and restore his standing among his kind. Then having lost the chess match to the unicorn, would no longer be of concern."

"Then why even bother with the chess match?" I asked. "Why not just offer to trade the lithium for the clocks? Wouldn't that be safer? Not that I doubt your ability to beat the two hundred years reigning chess champion, or anything."

At that point, the unicorn responded. "It is a matter of proper protocol. Per ages-old tradition, the reigning chess champion must play all requesting opponents, but the informal games do not actually count towards anything, other than amusement for the champion if you understand. If an opponent declares a formal challenge, then wagers are placed, the records keeper is called, and other formalities are invoked. If the Lithium is the wager, then the only way he could take it is by winning. If you were to simply approach him with an offer of trading the mineral for the clocks, he would most likely just seize the Lithium and be done with it. You would be very fortunate to get out with your heads intact, much less still attached. But as the basis of a championship game wager, he would not be able to touch it without winning."

"Well, a trade would certainly not work," Sherlock declared. "A chess match it is, or should I say several chess matches. I would like each of you who knows how to play chess, to request an informal game, so I can observe his style of play, and put a plan into effect. Most every player has a unique approach to the game, and while logic and analytical deduction, in which I am unmatched, are critical, having an idea of my opponent's strategy will help. So, who here knows how to play the King's Game?"

At that point, all of us raised our hands, indicating that we knew how to play, and the unicorn simply nodded and state, that while it too, was skilled in chess, the dragon might not be very acquiescent to playing against a unicorn again, even in an informal match. However, it did state that it could help in other ways suitable to its unique abilities and skills.

"Wonderful!" Sherlock replied. "How long do you think it will take you to acquire the Lithium, Miss Leeda? We will need a considerable quantity of it before we approach the creature."

At that point, first the unicorn, and then Miss Leeda disappeared as the creature whisked her away to procure the required element. In almost no time at all, they returned with a large burlap sack.

"What were you saying Mr. Holmes?" she asked. "I must say, that was the most marvelous experience of my life. I had no idea riding a unicorn could be so exhilarating! Getting there and back was almost instantaneous. The only part that took any time was negotiating with Dr. Matthiessen."

"If you call that negotiating!" The unicorn interrupted. "She can be most persuasive. I have never seen anything so effective in my entire existence, in this time period or my own."

"That may be," Sherlock stated, "but we must be on our way, as time is limited, and we must complete our task before the other organization realizes our presence and can intervene. They will not be happy when we succeed in recovering the clocks."

Turning to Miss Iris, Sherlock gathered detailed information on the whereabouts of the dragon, the surrounding area, and the opposing organization. Thus, armed with in-depth knowledge of their stronghold, a large bag of lithium, and what Sherlock described to us as, a sure-fire plan to reclaim the clocks, we were off. I could only hope that his sure-fire plan wasn't sure to get us roasted in the fire. And I am talking about dragon's fire.

Chapter 15.

Sherlock Comes up with an Idea as Clever as a Fox. (And that was before we even set off to encounter the dragon.)

We were off.

However, prior to leaving, a few significant items of interest did occur, which I should expound upon. First, I must apologize to our dear, Mrs. Hudson. Just as we were preparing to take the leap into the dragon's den, which had been described by Miss Iris as, "a horrible place of fire and ash," Mrs. Hudson had the unfortunate bad timing of bringing a tray of refreshments into the room asking if we would like some tea and hot *toast*. Needless to say, after our response, she may never bring us breakfast again.

Secondly, as part of his plan, Sherlock gathered two large framed mirrors, and carefully wrapped them for our journey.

Finally, I saw him whispering something to the unicorn. It was out of my hearing range, but he did have a rather devious and clever smile on his face.

Also, Miss Iris, since she had delivered the clocks to members of the organization at the den of the dragon, had described in detail, where the timepieces were being kept. It sounded like a cross between a scene from Dante's Inferno, and the inside of a blast furnace. The dragon kept all of the losers of championship matches chained to seats at a long table of chess boards. He kept them continually playing against him, while he traveled up and down the length of the table, rebuking and tormenting them with his fiery breath. There was a lone table with a board set up for anyone who cared to request an informal game, or for someone foolish enough to formally challenge him to a championship match. It sounded genuinely terrible and most befitting his name.

Lastly, in order to keep our identities hidden from any of the organization's members who may have seen us in Mr. Van der Lucht's flat, Sherlock provided disguises for all of us. Even Miss Iris was given a disguise. Since they only knew her as a soot-covered chimney sweep, the obvious choice was for her to simply change into a dress. I must say, she looked quite fetching, and I would have never recognized her from her previous appearance.

The unicorn was to provide our transportation one at a time to the exterior of the den, and then we would enter as a group while it remained invisible and ready to assist as required. I cannot say for sure, which I dreaded more, the dragon's den, or another terrifying, tree-dodging ride on a unicorn at speeds beyond imagination.

We safely arrived (even if I did get considerably closer to several trees than I would have ever imagined it possible to do and still live to tell about it) at the abandoned building that was serving as a den for Tourmaline the Terrible. It was on the outskirts of London, in a locale surrounded by bogs. The river had flooded the area sometime in the past and left it unusable for anything except concealing a dragon's den in the middle of Victorian England. The horrendous stench from the bogs was awful enough and kept everyone away, but the foul odors from the dragon's breath and his tendency to randomly shoot flames into the air at the slightest provocation made it even worse.

We were all assembled, and with no lack of trepidation, we entered the decrepit, decaying building. Other than the dragon and his "permanent" opponents, no one else was there. The members of the opposing organization were apparently off on some task. At first glance, the structure seemed as if it could collapse at any moment, but upon further examination, looked as if it might possibly hold up until we were finished with our task. It was dark, and the few flickering torches that were attached to the building's columns gave off a dim, weak light. The challenger's table was directly inside the entrance, while the long table with the remaining few unfortunate souls who had lost a championship match, was off to the left. The two men, still chained to their seats, were gaunt and haggard, dressed in tattered rags of what looked like at one time may have been fine clothes. A table with two ornate clocks that I recognized from the photo stood in the back of where Tourmaline was pacing up and down in front of the long "losers" table. As we entered, the dragon stopped in his tracks, turned towards us, and in a loud booming voice, spoke.

"What is this? Finally, some new challenges? It is about time. And not one, but two female chess players. This is most intriguing. What is the occasion, that not one, but five of you come at the same time to seek a game of chess against the centurys' long -reigning chess champion of the Mystical Realm? Speak, before I grow bored of you all."

And with that, he turned back to one of the two men quivering in fear, moved a golden bishop piece and exclaimed, "Checkmate you fool! That was not a game; that was pathetic! You have gotten worse over the last five years. What is with wrong with you?" He screeched, as he shot a small burst of flame above his opponent's quivering head.

Sherlock, now dressed in a deep-blue hooded robe, boldly stepped forward from the group and addressed the beast. "Tourmaline, the terrible-tempered, and largely lacking in hospitality, it may be that he has grown bored playing against such an ungracious host. The conditions here are appalling, not at all worthy of a chess champion that has reigned for over two hundred years. When was the last time anyone offered you a truly challenging game of chess? The conditions here are such, that if this were a raft in the middle of the ocean, one would rather drown then come aboard."

The dragon spun around, turned directly towards Holmes, lowered his head to Sherlock's eye level, and slowly asked, "What did you say? You would dare to address me in that way! I am the reigning champion, and the surrounding conditions are by my choice!"

Sherlock pointed at him, and replied, "That is because you despise your physical appearance, and you prefer the light in this place to be as low as possible, so as not to remind you of your lack of hue. You may be the champion in the game of kings, but in your appearance, you are but a knave. However, I, the great wizard Sherlock, have the solution! I can change your appearance, but only if you can beat me in a game of chess!"

The creature's eyes grew large, and it grinned a broad, toothy smile replying," What is this you say? Are you challenging me to a formal championship match, with your secret for modifying my appearance as the wager? How do I know you are telling the truth? I have known many wizards over the ages, and I have never heard of you."

Sherlock waved his hand, and the chess pieces on the challenger's board suddenly started to move as if of their own accord. I knew it was the unicorn, in its transparent state.

"Do not doubt my skills and abilities, Tourmaline the too confident. I can move the chess pieces merely by commanding them to do so. My skills are unmatched. No one even dares mention my name, or if they do, it is whispered in fear and respect. Regarding my ability to alter your appearance, let me give you a demonstration. A small sample of my power, so to speak."

Sherlock reached into his bag, and removed a large chunk of the Lithium element, unwrapped it from an oiled cloth, and held it up before the dragon.

"Behold, my creation!" He cried out, and then threw it towards the creature's mouth, saying, "Quick, swallow it!"

Without even thinking, Tourmaline snatched it from the air, and ingested it whole. "That is it?" the dragon asked skeptically. "I fail to see your power, and I am losing interest quickly."

Sherlock then indicated to Mr. Van der Lucht to uncover the mirrors he had brought with, and waved his hand saying, "Now let there be light!"

At that moment, the room somehow grew considerably brighter, and the dragon was able to see his reflection in the mirrors.

"It is not possible!" the creature exclaimed, seeing the reflected likeness of his entire head, and a large portion of his shoulder scales, now a vibrant metallic green. He stared intently at the image, obviously enjoying his appearance, for the first time, and asked. "How is it so? What exactly is it you wish to wager for?"

Sherlock waved his hand casually and replied. "It is my formula, a secret known by no one except me. If you wish to gain its gift, you will first play each of my assistants, informally, of course. Then you will play in a championship against me. And my choice for the wager is those two old clocks on the table behind you. A mere trifle for a secret so powerful that it will change your life forever. One that will restore your place in the realm of dragons."

Tourmaline hesitated a moment, and asked, "Those? They are not mine to wager. I am just watching over them for an associate, in return for a favor. Is there nothing else here of interest? I have many chess sets made of gold, silver, and even diamonds. Might they be something that could tempt you?"

Sherlock frowned. "It is the clocks or nothing. By the most ancient and honored rules and protocols of the Mystical Realm, the champion must accept a formal championship challenge, and the accompanying wager proposed. Or do you choose to forfeit? I stand ready to surrender myself and my formula, should I lose. The choice is yours!"

Chapter 16.

A Rather Rapid Series of Chess Games and Sherlock Sets the Stage for the Ultimate Endgame. (In retrospect, it was over before it even started.)

The dragon blew a long, steady stream of fire towards the ceiling above the challenger's table, gave a chilling tooth filled grin, and simply said, "I accept."

No sooner had the dragon stated his acceptance, then a gnomish looking figure, clutching a large and heavy leather bound book, popped out from behind the remains of a wall, proclaiming, "By the power vested in me by the Mystical Realm, I hereby record this match and the official wager that was agreed to seven seconds ago. The contestants will..."

"Not yet, you fool!" Tourmaline interrupted. I have to first dispose of these *informal* challengers." Then turning to our group, he added. "Not literally, I assure you." And returning his attention to the recorder, he continued. "Now be off, I will notify you when I have need of your services."

And with that, he blew a stream of flame to where the gnome who had vanished, had just been standing. "Now, where were we? Who would like to be my first victim? Figuratively, I assure you. Shall we start with ladies first?"

Miss Leeda stepped forward, and sat in the challenger's chair, resetting the pieces that had previously been mysteriously moved around the board.

"My name is Miss Leeda," she began, "Challenger takes white, or in this case, silver. You then will be gold."

Then turning her head to a slight angle, as if in examining the dragon in deep thought, she added, "If you don't mind me mentioning, I think you would look truly magnificent in gold. You really are a handsome creature. The wizard can do that, you know. King's pawn to King's pawn 4."

Taking his place at the board across from her, and moving his own King's pawn, Tourmaline beamed upon hearing Miss Leeda's compliment. "Really? You think I would look even more handsome in gold?" Then turning to Sherlock, he asked, "Wizard, is your secret formula veritably capable of changing my scales to golden?"

Sherlock, looked at him and responded, "Another demonstration? Why certainly!" And with that, he reached into his bag, withdrew a second block of Lithium, and threw it to the dragon, who almost upset the board as he snatched it from the air. Moments after swallowing the substance, his scales, from the level of his shoulders to several feet downward, took on a golden yellow hue.

"My, you certainly do look handsome." Miss Leeda replied moving another pawn. Although the dragon was somewhat distracted by his new appearance, and Miss Leeda was a strong player, the game concluded with Tourmaline winning.

"Thank you; it was a pleasure," she politely stated. "Believe it, or not this was my first time playing against a dragon."

Miss Leeda stepped away from the chess board, and Miss Iris took her place, introducing herself. "Good day, Sir Dragon. My name is Miss Iris."

The dragon exhaled a small puff of smoke, and grinning, asked, "Would you by any chance be a bearded Iris? I understand they are lovely flowers. Very popular with royalty."

Smiling coyly, while she reset the chess pieces, she responded, "Oh no, I am from the Netherlands, so that makes me a Dutch Iris. I did meet a Bearded Iris once though. She was one of the side-show oddities in the circus that the American fellow, P.T. Barnum brought to England. A charming lady actually. king's pawn to king's pawn 4."

Then looking intently at the fearsome beast, she added, "Truthfully though, I must say, I think you would look outstanding in silver. That is without question, the perfect color for your scales. I am sure that Wizard Sherlock would consider one more small example."

Tourmaline turned in the direction of Holmes only to see a medium-sized block of Lithium already heading towards him, which he eagerly snatched up and swallowed, immediately looking into the mirrors to see the anticipated change. Once again, his scales just below the area that was golden began to change in their appearance, taking on a glistening silver-grey color.

"Superlative!" the dragon exclaimed proudly admiring his reflection in the mirrors, "Simply superlative!"

With each following game, the dragon received an additional sample of Lithium, each time modifying the color of his scales until his coat was a veritable rainbow of green, gold, silver, red, blue, and black. With each improvement in the appearance of his coat, his playing grew increasingly careless. I will admit, that when I finally played against him, I honestly had to let myself lose, so as not to raise his suspicion. Sherlock even took advantage of the creature's preoccupation with his appearance to convince him to release the remaining two captives before giving Tourmaline the last demonstration of his "magic" formula. The two gentleman sincerely thanked Sherlock and hurried to exit the building before the dragon changed its mind.

At last, came the actual championship match, and the gnome reappeared, beginning his formal speech, "By the power vested in me by the Mystical Realm, I hereby record this match and the official wager that was agreed to thirty-five minutes, twenty-seven seconds ago. The contestants will..." However, at the moment in which he casually glanced up towards Tourmaline, resplendent in his shimmering, multi-colored coat of scales, the gnome abruptly stopped and stared wide-eyed at the brightly colored creature.

"Tourmaline? Is that you? My how you have changed! Did I miss something?"

The dragon, without taking his eyes off of his reflections in the mirrors, strategically positioned on each side of Sherlock responded proudly, "Yes, it is I, in all my new magnificence, and brilliance. Let us dispense with the formal funeral prose and begin the game."

And with that Sherlock waved his hand, and his king's pawn magically moved two spaces forward. Holmes then leaned forward to the dragon and inquired, "So tell me Tourmaline the tastefully versicolored, which color do you most prefer? They all make you look so radiant and regal."

Turning his head first to the left and then to the right as he intently gazed into the mirrors, Tourmaline haphazardly moved a pawn, and replied, "I am truthfully not certain. They all look so imposing and magnanimous; it is difficult to decide."

Sherlock casually waved his hand, and the queen's bishop silently moved to king's bishop four. "Yes, indeed, your coat is superlative and most striking. In fact, if you look closely into the mirrors, you can see the sublime richness of your scales as never before."

Without even looking at the board, Tourmaline moved his queen's rook's pawn one space forward, and replied, "Yes, yes. I see what you mean. Sublime richness does describe my coat very nicely.

Sherlock's queen subtly moved to King's rook five, and he continued in his praise of the dragon, "Without question, Tourmaline the Transcendent, your appearance is next to none. Never before has a dragon's coat been so peerless and preeminent. Just look at yourself in the mirrors. I must say, if the mirrors were alive and aware, they would be honored and humbled to reflect such greatness and perfection. You will be the envy of all dragon kind."

Paying little attention to the position of the pieces, Tourmaline quickly moved his king's knight to king's bishop three, and proudly proclaimed, "Yes, you are right. At last, I can return to my kind, and proclaim my greatness!"

Sherlock stood and replied, "Indeed you can Tourmaline the truly unequaled. There is no longer any reason for you to remain here. Your reign as chess champion is over, and your reign as the most handsome of all dragons has begun. Queen to king's bishop seven. Queen takes pawn. Your king is in checkmate! The game is over. Now you can proudly return to your realm in triumph. Your coat is incomparable!"

With a startled frown, the dragon quickly looked from the mirrors and stared intently at the board, and then stared at Sherlock with a wide grin." Yes, so it is checkmate. Cleverly done, Wizard. But you are correct. I can return to my own kind in triumph and take my place as the most handsome and incomparable dragon of all time." With a wide, curved gesture of his clawed hand, he swept the chess pieces from the board, and exclaimed, "Who needs any of this? After more than two hundred years, I was growing rather bored with chess. You can have the clocks. I am returning home!"

And with that the dragon exhaled a long stream of fire into the air, flapped his great wings and took off, flying through one of the windows with a thunderous resounding crash. We all watched in silence as the creature disappeared off into the distance.

The clock keeper, Van der Lucht was the first to speak, and he applauded as he exclaimed, "That was brilliant Mr. Holmes, simply brilliant. The dragon is gone. He neglected to attend to the clocks and left them behind, and we will still have enough time to bring the unicorns back."

Our happiness at the success of Sherlock's outrageous plan was quickly interrupted, when Miss Leeda suddenly pointed, and with great dismay, exclaimed, "But how can we do that? Look! The clocks are no longer on the table! They are gone!"

Chapter 17.

An Unexpected Return to the Case of the Missing Clocks.
(But this time, Sherlock has everything under control, and in
a timely manner.)

We all turned and looked where the clocks had last been,
and as she had stated, the table was empty. "What do we do
now?" exclaimed Van der Lucht. "This was our only chance!
Midnight is almost upon us.

Suddenly a new voice came out of the dim reaches of the
back of the room. "Yes Sherlock Holmes, what are you going
to do now?"

We all turned and saw several men, armed with small
crossbows, emerging from the shadows. One of them spoke
again. "It looks like we returned just in time. We have been
watching the clock keepers very closely over the years, and
we knew he would try something when we, at last, made our
move. When he contacted you, we expected trouble, which is
why we dispatched our sharpshooters to the keepers' flat. It
appears we underestimated you. I am surprised that you were

able to find this place, not to mention outwitting a dragon! I would have thought the beast would keep anyone away. Now tell me. What have you done with the clocks?"

At that point, both Miss Leeda and Van der Lucht interrupted. "But we don't have the clocks!"

Sherlock then took over and continued. "Yes, we were all watching the dragon fly away after he crashed through the window. We turned around, and they were gone, presumably more of your organization's misdoings. Now it is my turn to ask, what have you done with the clocks?"

Everyone there began looking around somewhat confused, pointing fingers, and talking all at once. It was slightly chaotic until Sherlock took out his revolver and fired it into the air to get everyone's attention. He then pocketed the gun, held his arms up in surrender and said, "It is obvious that we do not have the clocks. Feel free to search us. Will you allow us to do the same? Everyone present, both your group and ourselves, are here because of those mysterious, timeless clocks. Mr. Van der Lucht seeks to use them to return the first unicorn and its mate to Earth. While your organization seeks to prevent them from returning, and even to banish the unicorn living in Scotland to the heavens. Why is that, if I may ask? Why do you hate them so?"

The group's leader looked confused and was momentarily silent as he looked back and forth between his comrades, before he lowered his crossbow, and spoke. "That has been the sole objective of this organization since I was recruited and joined. That is the way it has been for centuries. I cannot say why. It just is. That's all there is to it. It just IS."

Sherlock casually removed a water canteen from the folds of his robe, took a swallow, offered it to the leader and replied. "It just is! I will drink to that. Please do join me. It is rather dry, hot and dusty in here. This place leaves a particularly foul taste in one's mouth. Do share the water with your companions. I assure you it is safe. You can see I drank it and am unaffected in any way." He casually handed the container to the leader of the group, who drank from it and shared it with his associates, commenting, "That was rather good. Quite refreshing actually."

Smiling and nodding, Sherlock continued. "The founder of your organization may have had her personal reason centuries ago. She was angry and bitter that the unicorns had left her for the sake of their own safety, but their lives depended on it. She was consumed by her anger and devoted her life to preventing their return. However, this fine gentleman and his organization have been dedicating their lives over the ages to preserving the machinations and methodology for them to return. Again, I ask you. Why would you seek to prevent them from returning? What is to be gained compared to what would be lost for eternity?"

The trio glanced around looking somewhat bewildered, stared down at the ground, and then finally looked straight at Sherlock, and sighed deeply as if a great weight had been lifted from their shoulders. "I don't know what we were thinking." The leader said, turning his head back and forth between his two associates, who were also looking embarrassed and nodding their heads in agreement. "I am sorry we can't help you. We honestly do not have the clocks. I can only wish you the best in recovering them. We will be off if you don't mind. This place is indeed rather depressing and foul."

And with that, they laid their crossbows down and silently left the building. Miss Leeda rushed up to Sherlock with tears in her eyes and grabbed his hand, shaking it vigorously. "That was profoundly stated, and beautifully put, Mr. Holmes. Should you ever decide to give up detective work, you could make a successful career in public speaking or politics."

I humorously replied, "Excuse me, but I have known Sherlock Holmes much longer than you, Miss Leeda, and I can honestly say, that he would rather take up crime than politics."

Mr. Van der Lucht, nervously looking at his pocket watch interrupted, "That may be, but what use is any of that? We still do not have the clocks, and time is running out. We must perform the procedure by midnight tonight, or all is lost."

Sherlock raised a hand and simply stated. "Well then, let us be off. I assure you, the clocks are safely waiting for us with Miss Iris, in Mrs. Hudson's garden at Baker Street.

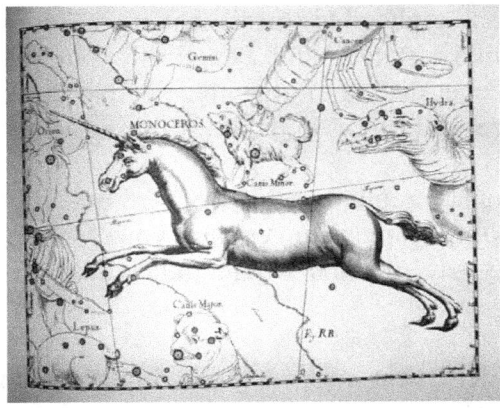

Chapter 18

A Long Awaited Return. (And several even longer over-due explanations.)

I looked around us and suddenly realized that indeed Miss Iris was nowhere to be seen. I had not even noticed her disappearance until Sherlock had mentioned it. I was about to question him, when the unicorn suddenly rematerialized in our midst and stated. "If I may say so, Wizard Holmes, your plan to outwit the dragon by using his vanity, (dragons really are such vain creatures.) and to overcome our opponents the way you did, came off like clockwork, if you will pardon the expression, primarily utilizing the healing water that I provided. That was exceptionally clever of you. I was not confident you would be able to convince them to drink it. I knew that any water touched by my alicorn could heal their long-held negative emotions. However, getting it inside of them is another matter entirely.

Miss Leeda burst into laughter and exclaimed, "So that was it! Yes, you would certainly make an excellent politician. You are more than convincing and conniving enough."

"But it was for a good cause," Sherlock replied. "Now let us quickly return to Baker Street!"

And one by one we were whisked away by the unicorn at speeds I would prefer to forget, but am most assuredly not likely to, considering the number of trees I am on personal terms with. Even if the unicorn says, there was more than a hair's breadth between us and the tree.

When we had all safely returned, (and "safely" is a relative term, as I still have nightmares about traveling at impossible speeds with trees jumping directly in front of me.), we all gathered in Mrs. Hudson's garden, and indeed, as Sherlock had stated, there were the two clocks.

Average in size for a mantel clock, they were finely carved of varnished cherry wood, with intricate ivory unicorns inlaid into the sides. The clock faces were inscribed with arcane and abstruse astronomical images and figures, and both featured the constellation Monoceros in the center of the dial. Each timepiece was sitting on a small marble table at opposite ends of the enclosed garden space, and Mr. Van der Lucht was tremblingly examining them in detail. "Thank goodness! They seem to be intact. They do not seem to have been damaged in any way, and most importantly, the internal crystals are still there. I can begin the process to return the unicorns to Earth."

He then paced off the distance between the two clocks, adjusting them slightly. He used the small telescope that was incorporated into the cap of his walking stick to look up into the night sky, consulted a pocket compass, and made additional minor adjustments to the exact positions of the devices, and then wound both the clocks. Satisfied with their arrangement, he carefully reached into his leather bag, which he had retrieved from his flat on his way back from the dragon's den and removed two delicately small, pure white unicorn figurines. Their detail was incredible, and they were beautiful beyond description. I had never before seen such life-like carvings if indeed that is what they were. He carefully placed them on the ground centered between the two clocks and stepping backward, glanced at his pocket watch. He looked at us all and said, "It is almost time."

Staring intently at his watch, while snatching glances up into the night sky, he approached the clock on the left and stood with his hand poised over a lever on the side of the device. Almost quivering with apprehension, he counted down to the beginning of the process, "Three, two, one," and switched the lever on the first clock, starting the mechanism. He then briskly walked over to the second clock and held his hand over the similar lever on that device. After what seemed like an eternity, he once again counted down, "Three, two, one," and threw the switch activating it.

Not knowing what to expect, we were all breathless in anticipation as the two ornate chronographs slowly ticked the seconds off. Stepping away from them while glancing back and forth, between the two timepieces, and his pocket watch, he again began a countdown, "Three, two, one, now!"

Just as he finished speaking, in the distance, Big Ben's tower clock bell began striking the hour of midnight, and the strangest thing occurred. Both of the unicorn clocks started running backward. Slowly at first, the second, minute, and hour hands were turning counter-clockwise, but they gathered speed and soon were rapidly spinning around the dial. As they did, the two unicorn figurines began to glow, and somehow it seemed as if they were increasing in size. Ever so slightly at first, and then brighter and brighter until the garden was painted with a sparkling brilliance that filled the night air around us. As the radiance increased, so did their height and width. Soon they were full-sized statues, glowing brightly. We all held our breath and looked at each other expectantly, but then it all just stopped,

The clocks had stopped ticking, and the luminous glow faded into the night. In the darkness and silence that lingered, all that remained were two remarkably lifelike, full-sized statues of unicorns.

Crestfallen, Van der Lucht, stared wide-eyed in surprise and disappointment, and turned to the group and uttered, "Well? Well? That's it? There has to be more! This cannot be the end. It has to work! It simply must work! After all these years, and centuries. It cannot fail..."

We were all standing in uncertain silence, when Miss Iris slowly pointed towards the statues and asked. "Is it my imagination, or does it look like that statue may be breathing?"

"You are right!" exclaimed Miss Leeda, "They are breathing!"

Impossible as it seemed, we could feel the slight breaths that appeared to come from them, and see their long manes begin to flutter in the faint breeze. Once again, they began to glimmer, and glow, and then it was as if a thin surface shell started to fall away from them in bits and pieces, revealing a pure white luminosity that was increasing with each second. Finally, in one blinding flash of light, the exterior shells exploded sending fragments in all directions, and we turned our heads to the side to avoid the flying shards.

When it had all faded away, and we turned to again look where they had been, there now stood two magnificent living unicorns. They had at last returned.

Chapter 19.

At Long Last, the First Unicorn. (And we all second that.)

The creatures were the very physical embodiment of beauty and perfection. They cast a warm, luminous radiance that permeated the night, and their alicorns were spiral horns of light that somehow, shone even brighter. The larger and more muscular of the two, the male, first tapped the ground with one hoof, as if feeling the soft damp earth, then reared up pawing at the sky, in celebration, while the smaller and more petite looking female shook herself all over as if to embrace the sensation of once again being in a physical form. They slowly approached each other, first lightly touching their alicorns together, and then gently nuzzling their muzzles in a loving caress. I could almost feel their joy at being able to physically embrace after more than two centuries of being close together in non-corporeal forms.

After cuddling, they slowly looked about the garden taking it all in, and abruptly stopped when they saw the unicorn clocks.

The keeper, Van der Lucht cautiously approached them and was the first to speak. "Yes, these are the timepieces that were used to send your spirits to the heavens so many years ago. They have been preserved and protected, over the centuries so you could once again return to Earth as was planned, but it almost did not happen. Van den Keere's wife, Anna Beurt was so distraught when you both left, that she formed a group dedicated over the years to prevent your return, and they stole the chronographs. Sherlock Holmes, Dr. Watson, and these two fine ladies worked together and recovered the clocks, and he even outwitted a dragon to make it possible for you both to be here."

The larger of the two unicorns nodded its head, and replied in a voice as old as time, "A dragon. That would have to be Tourmaline the Terrible. He never did forgive me for beating him in that chess match. His vanity will someday be his downfall."

The female unicorn, gazed towards us and in a soft, delicate voice, somewhat akin to a wind chime, said, "Thank you for all of your efforts. We are most grateful to you. It is good to be here, to be home, but then the heavens have been our home for so long, a part of us remains up there. We will always be connected to the Monoceros constellation. And someday we will return to it. It is our legacy, and in it remains the spirits of our offspring."

The male unicorn added, "From our place in the stars, we have been observing humanity over the centuries. You have grown and matured, but so many of you have also lost your sense of wonder, and your connection to the Mystical Realm. Will this era be any less dangerous for us? Was it worth the effort and sacrifice to be away so long?"

Then looking at the unicorn that had accompanied us back from Camelot and started this entire adventure, he continued, "I see that there is at least one unicorn in this age."

The unicorn bowed its head formally, and replied, "I am in truth not from the present. I am from the era of King Arthur in the 5th century. I came through a portal in the standing stones, forward into this time period, to discover what had become of you and your mate. When you both disappeared without a trace in the 1600's, every unicorn throughout all eternity felt the void created by your absence. I vowed to discover what had become of you and solve the mystery of the first unicorn, but I could not do it alone. Sherlock Holmes is unequaled in solving the unsolvable, and revealing the unknown, and he agreed to help solve this, the greatest of all mysteries."

"Their arrival was most opportune," Van der Lucht interjected, "as they appeared just in time to recover the chronographs required to bring you back before the deadline passed."

Miss Leeda gratefully added, "All that matters, is that you are both here, and the world is now a better place because of it!" We all nodded our heads in agreement and seconded her statement.

The first unicorn then tossed his head, with his silken main fluttering, and replied, "Yes, we are at long last here. We will go and experience this new and different world that we have returned to, but as my loving mate stated, someday we must

113

return again to the stars, and take our places in the Monoceros Constellation. We will need someone to continue to watch over the unicorn clocks until that time."

In unison, Van der Lucht and Miss Iris both exclaimed, "I will!" Then they gazed at each other, smiled, reached out to hold each other's hands, and said, "*We* will."

The female unicorn approached them, lightly touched her alicorn to each of their foreheads, and said, "So it is."

The first unicorn crossed over to his mate, deftly brushed against her, turned to look at us and said, "Once more, we extend our gratitude to all of you, I am sure we will meet again."

And with that they left the garden, and vanished into the night, leaving a lingering warmth and glow that slowly faded away.

We all stood for a moment in silence and the realization that we had indeed succeeded, and the first unicorns had returned to our world. It would indeed be a better place because of our efforts.

I then turned to Sherlock, and commented, "You do realize, Holmes, that this makes it twice in a row now, you have used 'the Scholar's four-move Mate' to win a game of chess on which our very lives depended. Managing to pull it off once, in Camelot, was impressive, but using that approach to defeat the reigning chess champion of over two hundred years was a bit risky, I think."

"You see, but you do not observe, Watson." He replied. "In both matches, I had learned all I needed to know to defeat

114

them just by observing the finer details of their characters and personalities. Miss Iris's description of Tourmaline was so clear and accurate that I knew that by using his vanity against him I could defeat him with my eyes closed."

"What does, having your eyes closed, have to do with it?" I answered. "You are also an expert in blindfold chess. You don't even need to see the board to play. You can memorize the exact position of every piece on the board and easily win."

Sherlock shrugged his shoulders. "Well yes, that is true. I should write a monograph on that someday, but the important fact is that I learned what I needed to know through precise observation of the unnoticed and minute finer details. I even wrote a monograph on the subject. '*A Guide to...*'"

"Yes, you have mentioned that one before, on more than one occasion, I believe."

The unicorn stamped its hoof and interrupted. "What does it matter? It is done! Not only is the mystery of the first unicorn finally solved, but they have also returned to Earth. And I assisted in the course of action. Who could have imagined? Now I can now return to my own time knowing that my quest is successfully completed. Thank you all, and especially thank you, Wizard Holmes. You will be remembered in the authenticated, and sanctioned chronicles of unicorns for all eternity."

The unicorn reared up on its hind legs, struck a regal pose for just a moment, and vanished.

The clock keeper Van der Lucht turned to Sherlock and shook his hand vigorously, saying, "Yes, Mr. Holmes, you will also be remembered in our histories. My centuries-old secret task is finally over. And now we have a new purpose, to keep and protect the clocks for the unicorns' eventual return to the heavens. We will never forget this night."

"We?" I asked, curiously.

He then gently took Miss Iris's hand and said, "Yes, Anna Beurt's group has been dissolved, so Miss Iris no longer has a real home to live in. I have invited her to stay in my assistant's room, and she has agreed. He had always said, that once we had completed our task to safely return the unicorns, he wanted to leave London and travel the world, so his room will now be available.

Miss Iris added, "And we both have so much in common. Having surreptitiously gained entrance to his domicile twice, I already am very familiar with his home. I can easily return the clocks to exactly where I found them. They will be a fond memory of this special night."

They both said their goodbyes to us and left together, each cradling one of the two timepieces that had been so instrumental in this strange and unusual adventure.

Miss Leeda brushed off her dress, and said, "Well, I need to collect my bag and return to my lodgings. Tomorrow I will be off to Scotland. There is a great deal of fieldwork there for me to finish, and some very healing and rejuvenating waters will also be there if I am not mistaken. This has been a most prodigious and unforgettable experience. When I sought to engage your services to recover my journal, Mr. Holmes, I had no idea where it would lead to." Then looking directly at me, she coyly added, "But I must say, am certainly glad it did."

Taking the opportunity, I offered to walk her back to her hotel, especially since it was already so late at night, and not safe for a woman to be walking all alone in the streets of London. She did remind me that she was skilled in a goodly number of self-defense and fighting skills and that her handbag contained several more ways to stop an attacker cold in his tracks, but she still thanked me and welcomed my companionship on the journey back.

She bid Sherlock farewell and expressed her gratitude to him for recovering her journal and bag of crystals, and though it was late and rather cold, we slowly walked arm in arm back to her hotel, very much enjoying every moment of our brief time together. I assured her that we would most certainly meet again, very soon, but considering the events of the last several days, I found myself wondering if indeed we would, and hoping that it might in some way be possible. My confidence was bolstered, when she kissed me goodbye and pressed into my hand, a unique and beautiful crystal saying, "Have faith, Dr. Watson, this will lead you back to me."

Chapter 20.

A Most Strange and Challenging Invitation, (If it could be called that at all.)

When I returned to our flat later that night, I was quite ready for a much-needed nip of brandy and my comfortable bed and was looking forward to both. I did not, however, expect to find Sherlock pacing back and forth in the study with his coat and deerstalker hat on, apparently waiting for me.

"Don't bother removing your coat, Watson. We must be off promptly. Our services are required immediately." He waved a hand-written letter at me. "And make sure you bring along your service revolver."

"Are you serious?" I exclaimed. "What on Earth could be so important that we need to leave at this ungodly hour?"

He stopped his pacing, and handed me the letter, and said, "This!"

The printing looked something as though a deranged chicken had walked through an ink puddle and then run across the page. I cringed at the thought of who could have possibly written it. With some degree of hesitation, I read the note out loud and could not believe my eyes.

"To: Mr. Sherlock Holmes, Consulting Detective, and Dr. John Watson M.D.

"Your reputations precede you, and as such, there is no one other than yourselves who can assist me in this matter.

"I am on the verge of an achievement that will rewrite history, revolutionize science, and change the way humanity views the past. The event is close at hand, and your finely focused, calibrated, and objective eye that misses nothing must be present to witness the result and verify its validity.

"Also, do bring along your scribe, Dr. Watson, to record this event. His skills with a firearm and/or as a surgeon may be required.

"It is imperative that you meet me at the below address at 6 a.m. today. The fate of the entire world depends on it.

"Professor George Edward Challenger.
 F.R.S.,
M.D.,
D.Sc."

Coming soon!

Book one of the
Sherlock Holmes and the Missing Scientists
Trilogy:

Sherlock Holmes and the Adventure of the
Demonstrative Dinosaur

Also from Joseph Svec

The Missing Authors Series

 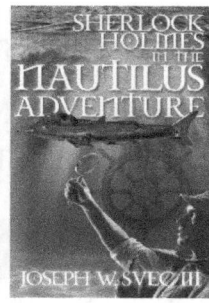 

Sherlock Holmes and The Adventure of The Grinning Cat
Sherlock Holmes and The Nautilus Adventure
Sherlock Holmes and The Round Table Adventure

"Joseph Svec, III is brilliant in entwining two endearing and enduring classics of literature, blending the factual with the fantastical; the playful with the pensive; and the mischievous with the mysterious. We shall, all of us young and old, benefit with a cup of tea, a tranquil afternoon, and a copy of Sherlock Holmes, The Adventure of the Grinning Cat."
Amador County Holmes Hounds Sherlockian Society

Also from MX Publishing

MX Publishing is the world's largest specialist Sherlock Holmes publisher, with over a hundred titles and fifty authors creating the latest in Sherlock Holmes fiction and non-fiction.

From traditional short stories and novels to travel guides and quiz books, MX Publishing cater for all Holmes fans.

The collection includes leading titles such as *Benedict Cumberbatch In Transition* and *The Norwood Author* which won the 2011 Howlett Award (Sherlock Holmes Book of the Year).

MX Publishing also has one of the largest communities of Holmes fans on Facebook with regular contributions from dozens of authors.

www.mxpublishing.com

Also from MX Publishing

Our bestselling books are our short story collections;

'Lost Stories of Sherlock Holmes' , 'The Outstanding Mysteries of Sherlock Holmes', The Papers of Sherlock Holmes Volume 1 and 2, 'Untold Adventures of Sherlock Holmes' (and the sequel 'Studies in Legacy) and 'Sherlock Holmes in Pursuit', 'The Cotswold Werewolf and Other Stories of Sherlock Holmes' – and many more……

www.mxpublishing.com

Also from MX Publishing

"Phil Growick's, 'The Secret Journal of Dr Watson', is an adventure which takes place in the latter part of Holmes and Watson's lives. They are entrusted by HM Government (although not officially) and the King no less to undertake a rescue mission to save the Romanovs, Russia's Royal family from a grisly end at the hand of the Bolsheviks. There is a wealth of detail in the story but not so much as would detract us from the enjoyment of the story. Espionage, counter-espionage, the ace of spies himself, double-agents, double-crossers...all these flit across the pages in a realistic and exciting way. All the characters are extremely well-drawn and Mr Growick, most importantly, does not falter with a very good ear for Holmesian dialogue indeed. Highly recommended. A five-star effort."
The Baker Street Society

www.mxpublishing.com

Also from MX Publishing

The American Literati Series

The Final Page of Baker Street
The Baron of Brede Place
Seventeen Minutes To Baker Street

"The really amazing thing about this book is the author's ability to call up the 'essence' of both the Baker Street 'digs' of Holmes and Watson as well as that of the 'mean streets' of Marlowe's Los Angeles. Although none of the action takes place in either place, Holmes and Watson share a sense of camaraderie and self-confidence in facing threats and problems that also pervades many of the later tales in the Canon. Following their conversations and banter is a return to Edwardian England and its certainties and hope for the future. This is definitely the world before The Great War."
Philip K Jones

www.mxpublishing.com

125

Also from MX Publishing

The Detective and The Woman Series

The Detective and The Woman
The Detective, The Woman and The Winking Tree
The Detective, The Woman and The Silent Hive

"The book is entertaining, puzzling and a lot of fun. I believe the author has hit on the only type of long-term relationship possible for Sherlock Holmes and Irene Adler. The details of the narrative only add force to the romantic defects we expect in both of them and their growth and development are truly marvelous to watch. This is not a love story. Instead, it is a coming-of-age tale starring two of our favorite characters."
Philip K Jones

Also from MX Publishing

When the papal apartments are burgled in 1901, Sherlock Holmes is summoned to Rome by Pope Leo XII. After learning from the pontiff that several priceless cameos that could prove compromising to the church, and perhaps determine the future of the newly unified Italy, have been stolen, Holmes is asked to recover them. In a parallel story, Michelangelo, the toast of Rome in 1501 after the unveiling of his Pieta, is commissioned by Pope Alexander VI, the last of the Borgia pontiffs, with creating the cameos that will bedevil Holmes and the papacy four centuries later. For fans of Conan Doyle's immortal detective, the game is always afoot. However, the great detective has never encountered an adversary quite like the one with whom he crosses swords in "The Vatican Cameos.."

"An extravagantly imagined and beautifully written Holmes story"
(**Lee Child**, NY Times Bestselling author, Jack Reacher series)

Also from MX Publishing

The Conan Doyle Notes (The Hunt For Jack The Ripper)
"Holmesians have long speculated on the fact that the Ripper
murders aren't mentioned in the canon, though the obvious
reason is undoubtedly the correct one: even if Conan Doyle
had suspected the killer's identity he'd never have considered
mentioning it in the context of a fictional entertainment. Ms
Madsen's novel equates his silence with that of the dog in the
night-time, assuming that Conan Doyle did know who the
Ripper was but chose not to say – which, of course, implies
that good old stand-by, the government cover-up. It seems
unlikely to me that the Ripper was anyone famous or
distinguished, but fiction is not fact, and "The Conan Doyle
Notes" is a gripping tale, with an intelligent, courageous and
very likable protagonist in DD McGil."
The Sherlock Holmes Society of London